TRAIL'S END FOR
THE TRAILSMAN

As he stood on the gallows platform with a rope around his neck, Skye Fargo snuck his hand down toward the Arkansas toothpick concealed in his ankle holster.

"We had to take this little knife off you, Mr. Fargo," the sheriff said, swinging the throwing knife in front of his eyes.

That cut it. Fargo felt the cool breeze against his sweaty face, the warmth of the sun on his shoulders. Many a time he'd faced down death and won. But now death finally had the upper hand.

"Any last words?" the sheriff said impatiently. Fargo heard the creak of the trapdoor below him. In a moment they'd pull the lever and he'd drop into space. If he was lucky, his neck would break and the end would be quick.

"Yeah," Fargo said. "You're hanging the wrong man."

The answer came quick. Fargo felt the boards give way beneath him. He felt himself dropping, down, down, the thick rough rope around his neck tightening.

Nothing could save him now. . . .

**Be sure to read the other novels in the
exciting Trailsman series!**

**FROM SPUR AWARD-WINNING
WESTERN WRITER**

SUZANN LEDBETTER

TRINITY STRIKE

From the heart of Ireland comes the irrepressible Megan
O'Malley, whose own spirit mirrors that of the untamed
frontier. With nothing to her name but fierce determina-
tion, Megan defies convention and sets out to strike it rich,
taking any job—from elevator operator to camp cook—to
get out west and become a prospector. In a few short
months, she has her very own stake in the Trinity mine—
and the attention of more than a few gun-slinging bandits.
But shrewd, unscrupulous enemies are lurking, waiting to
steal her land—and any kind of courtship must wait. . . .

from Signet

Prices slightly higher in Canada.   (0-451-18644-3—$5.50)

THE TRAILSMAN

172

SUTTER'S SECRET

by

Jon Sharpe

A SIGNET BOOK

SIGNET
Published by the Penguin Group
Penguin Books USA Inc., 375 Hudson Street,
New York, New York 10014, U.S.A.
Penguin Books Ltd, 27 Wrights Lane,
London W8 5TZ, England
Penguin Books Australia Ltd, Ringwood,
Victoria, Australia
Penguin Books Canada Ltd, 10 Alcorn Avenue,
Toronto, Ontario, Canada M4V 3B2
Penguin Books (N.Z.) Ltd, 182–190 Wairau Road,
Auckland 10, New Zealand

Penguin Books Ltd, Registered Offices:
Harmondsworth, Middlesex, England

First published by Signet, an imprint of Dutton Signet,
a division of Penguin Books USA Inc.

First Printing, April, 1996
10 9 8 7 6 5 4 3 2 1

The first chapter of this book originally appeared in *Dead Man's River*,
the one hundred seventy-first volume in this series.

REGISTERED TRADEMARK—MARCA REGISTRADA

Printed in the United States of America

The Trailsman

Beginnings . . . they bend the tree and they mark the man. Skye Fargo was born when he was eighteen. Terror was his midwife, vengeance his first cry. Killing spawned Skye Fargo, ruthless, cold-blooded murder. Out of the acrid smoke of gunpowder still hanging in the air, he rose, cried out a promise never forgotten.

The Trailsman they began to call him all across the West: searcher, scout, hunter, the man who could see where others only looked, his skills for hire but not his soul, the man who lived each day to the fullest, yet trailed each tomorrow. Skye Fargo, the Trailsman, and the seeker who could take the wildness of a land and the wanting of a woman and make them his own.

Hell's Picket, Wyoming Territory, 1860—
a two-bit town where frontier justice is swift,
and the noose is always ready to swing a man . . .
even the wrong one.

1

He'd seen worse.

The tall man reined in the black-and-white pinto at the top of a red bluff and sat looking down on the settlement. A couple dozen shacks and false-fronted lumber buildings stood below in the middle of the dry sage plain. The afternoon sun gilded the tin roofs, and they glistened like gold. Even from this distance, he could see tiny figures, wagons, and horses raising small plumes of dust in the wide streets. The winding red trail led into town and out again, away into the distance.

So, this was Hell's Picket. Yeah, in all his years riding the West, he'd seen a lot of shabby towns thrown up in the middle of nowhere. And he'd seen worse. His lake blue eyes swept the horizon, taking in the rosy bluffs and distant peaks. Far above in the crystal sky, a silent eagle floated. He felt the tug of the open trail, the empty wild land that lay all around. As if reading his thoughts, the Ovaro shifted beneath him and stamped a hoof impatiently.

Fargo stroked the Ovaro's strong neck. We have

a job to do, he told the animal silently. He pulled out a scrap of paper from his jacket pocket and reread the message that had somehow managed to reach him when he had been passing through Kansas City.

Mr. Fargo, it read. *I heard about you from Major Jake Lewis. He said you were the one if I ever needed help. I need it now. This thing's got too big for me and my boys to handle. If you can come, I'll meet you in Hell's Picket in Wyoming Territory on the first of July. Ask for Mack in the main hotel at sundown. I'll be able to pay you well.*

What the hell was it all about? Fargo had wondered. Who was this Mack character? And what was this about "my boys"? It sounded like a gang or a posse. His suspicions aroused, Fargo had sent off a telegram to his old friend Jake Lewis at Fort Reliance. But word came back that the major had got himself killed in Indian action the week before. And with Major Lewis dead, there was no way to find out anything about this mysterious message. Now there was only one thing to do. He had to go see for himself.

The pinto started forward on the trail heading into town. Beside the trail Fargo read the battered sign: WELCOME TO HELL'S PICKET, POPULATION 134 LAW-ABIDING CITIZENS. Fargo slowed the pinto to a canter and then to a walk as they reached the first buildings. Lining the dusty streets were the usual collection of storefronts: Emporium with trail supplies and groceries, Livery Stables, Sheriff's Office and Courthouse, and a store that promised "Tables, Chairs, Beds, and Coffins—Made to Order."

Mountain wagons rumbled by, loaded with kegs and boxes of supplies as well as piles of sheepskins and buffalo pelts. The drivers in their dusty clothes glanced at him curiously, their faces deep scored by sun and weather. There were few women around, and those he saw were dressed in homespun and hand-fashioned bonnets to keep off the harsh sun. Ranching life was hard hereabouts. A family could scrape a living out of the cruel land, Fargo knew, but the reward for their hard work could rarely be counted in greenbacks.

A pudgy red-faced man was passing out handbills to passersby. He ran puffing toward Fargo and reached up, offering him one.

"We got a shootin' show in the main square this afternoon!" the man said. "A world famous shootist—"

Fargo shook his head and refused the handbill, riding on. He'd seen real shooting enough for a lifetime. And most professional shootists were nothing more than circus performers, magicians, and charlatans, their supposedly deadeye aim depending more on props and tricks than real shooting skill. There were very few exceptions.

He reached the center of town to find an open square fronted by the large, ramshackle two-story Hell's Picket Hotel and Saloon. In the middle of the dusty square, Fargo noticed an elaborate platform, elevated ten feet above the ground with a wooden stair ascending. He could see the outlines of trapdoors in the platform. Above was the thick wood-beam arm of the gallows, and a couple of empty nooses swung in the breeze. He calculated there was room enough to hang half a dozen men at a time. Yeah, with that hanging stage looking at you every day, a man would sure stay law-abiding, he thought.

He dismounted and tethered his pinto in front of the hotel. A building on the far side of the square caught his eye. It was all gingerbread gables and filigreed shutters, garishly painted in bright pink and yellow. For a moment Fargo smiled in anticipation, thinking it must be a fancy bordello, but then he saw the windows were boarded over and the front door closed. The sign, SAM BLADE'S CASINO, swung by one nail. Businesses came and went on the frontier. Fargo idly wondered what had happened to that one.

" 'Scuse me, stranger," a deep voice said. Fargo turned to find himself face-to-face with a lanky fellow. His face was long and serious, and his skin hung in loose folds like an old dog's. A silver star was pinned to his leather vest.

"You must be sheriff of Hell's Picket," Fargo said, touching the brim of his hat.

"I am," the man said, not unfriendly, but without a smile. "And who might you be?"

"Name's Skye Fargo."

The sheriff looked him over twice.

"I've heard of you," he said. Still no smile. "What brings you to town?"

Even though he had nothing to hide, Fargo didn't like questions. There was no telling who this Mack character was or what he was getting himself into. Instinct told him to say as little as possible before he found out the whole story.

"Just passing through," Fargo answered lightly, without hesitation.

"Hm," the sheriff muttered and nodded, his eyes still on Fargo.

"Why all the questions?" Fargo asked. "You expecting some trouble around here?"

"Nope," the sheriff said. "I just like to keep my eye on any strangers coming through. We're a law-abiding town. Like to keep it that way."

"Sounds good to me," Fargo said agreeably.

The sheriff seemed to relax at this and offered his hand.

"The name's Harry Sikes," he said. They shook.

"Nice place," Fargo said, glancing around the square. "What happened to your casino over there?" He pointed across the way to the gaudy pink and yellow building.

"Oh, a fellow named Sam Blade came into town and opened up that big place," Sheriff Sikes explained. "Did right well for a spell. Got a lot of gambling men coming through, some new fancy girls, that kind of a thing. No trouble though. Well-run place. Then the rumor went around that the tables were fixed and the game was crooked. Well, I say a man's not guilty till you prove it. And nobody ever rightly caught Sam Blade cheating anybody. But I guess those gamblers felt like they were losing too often, and the gaming just dried up and went out of town again. Sam Blade went belly-up and left six months ago. We ain't seen him since."

A sudden commotion erupted at the other end of the street, and Fargo turned to see a figure riding hell-bent on a glistening palomino, both hands in the air, pistols blazing. The sheriff jumped and started to draw his gun.

"Oh hell, it's that shooting show," he said, jamming his gun back in his holster. He hurried away to the far side of the square. Fargo watched as the rider galloped with blurring speed expertly around the common, firing into the sky and shrieking like the very devil, as the citizens of Hell's Picket came running from all directions, shouting with excitement. Fargo grinned as he recognized Deadeye Dena. Hell, she was getting old, but still up to her old tricks.

Suddenly, the whole town seemed to take on the atmosphere of a carnival as the crowd gathered and the palomino raced around and around. Deadeye Dena whooped and stood on the saddle of her horse, holding the reins in one hand and firing into the air with the other. Then she reined in next to the gallows platform, and a cloud of dust swirled around her. When it cleared, she was standing on the platform, and Fargo got a good look at her.

It had been a few years since he'd run into Deadeye Dena, the Fastest Lady Shootist in the West. She hadn't changed a bit. Under her battered black hat, her sunburnt wrinkled face was as tough as old leather, and two silver braids hung down her back. Traces of her Shoshoni heritage showed in her strong jaw and her black eyes. She was wearing a buckskin-fringed dress on her wiry figure and silver-chased rattlesnake skin boots. Around her hips hung half a dozen holster belts with pistols of all kinds, and two bullet-filled bandoliers crossed her chest.

Dena gave a blood-curdling war whoop and doffed her black hat, tossing it in the air. She spun all the way around while she drew two long-barreled Vaquero pistols and plugged the hat a dozen times. It fluttered to the ground, cut neatly in two pieces while the crowd cheered.

"Betcha can't do that with a nickel!" a tall man in the crowd shouted to her. "Everybody knows women can't shoot."

"Got a nickel?" she said, her hand on one hip. "For every nickel I plug, you owe me one. For every nickel I miss, I give you two! And if you want to hop up here, I'll give you five nickels for every one you hit."

"Sold!" he said. The crowd laughed, eager to see the contest. The tall man climbed up the stairs and stood on the high gallows platform. He towered over the small figure of Deadeye Dena, and she smiled up at him with all the sweetness of a rattler about to strike.

Fargo stood at the back of the crowd and watched as the tall man tossed nickels high in the air and Dena plugged them, one by one, without fail. At first the man laughed as he handed over a nickel for every one she hit, but then his face became serious.

"It ain't so hard," he said, pulling out his gun. "Toss a few for me, and I'll show you how it's done."

Dena bent down and took a handful of nickels from her pile. She made sure he was ready, then tossed the first. It flew upward, high in the afternoon sky, glinting in the light. The tall man pulled the trigger, and the coin fell to earth. The crowd made a circle around it.

"Ain't hit it," somebody said, tossing the coin back to Dena.

"Want to try again?" she asked. He tried three more times with no better luck. He was sweating. Then he threw nickels into the air for her again, and, as the pile of nickels at her feet grew and he ran out of coins, the pile turned into greenbacks, and he grew restless. He shook his head as if giving up. The crowd egged him on.

"Come on, Marvin!" one of the men shouted. "Her luck's gotta turn soon!" But Fargo knew it was more than luck. It was skill. Deadeye Dena had spent her lifetime looking down the barrel of a gun or a pistol, and she could outshoot almost anybody in the West. Finally, the tall rancher had had enough.

"I quit!" he yelled, stomping off to the laughter of the crowd. "Must be some kind of a trick!"

Dena laughed too as she watched him go. Then she pulled a small hand mirror from her pocket. She turned her back to the retreating man and looked over her shoulder at his reflection in the mirror. Slowly, she raised her pistol and laid the barrel on her shoulder. A murmur went up from the crowd, a few men grumbled, the women gasped.

"Don't," somebody said softly. The sheriff, standing to one side, started forward as if to stop her.

Dena pulled the trigger. Across the square the tall man's hat flew off his head. He gave a yell and started to run, then turned back in a fury when he heard the crowd's laughter. He picked up his hat, beat the dust out of it and disappeared around a corner.

"Anybody else care to try?" Deadeye Dena asked. There was a silence in the crowd. Nobody wanted to take her on. Dena glanced at the pile of money at her feet, and Fargo read her thoughts in her face. That was all the money she'd make on this show. The crowd started to drift away as Dena bent down to gather up the bills and coins.

"Sure, I'll take you on," Fargo said.

Dena glanced up at the sound of his voice, and her face broke out in a big smile.

"Why, bless my bullets!" she said. "If it isn't Mr. Skye Fargo!" At the sound of his name, many in the crowd craned their necks, looking at him curiously, muttering among themselves. His name and reputation had spread throughout the West. "What brings you to Hell's Picket?"

"Just looking for something to shoot at!" Fargo said with a big smile on his face as he climbed the stairs to the platform. "You care to take me on?" The crowd applauded.

"I'll play you plugged pennies for gold eagles," Fargo offered. Dena whistled.

"Gold eagles? You devil," she said. "You're on."

"I'm bettin' on Fargo!" a man in the crowd called out.

"Not me," another said. "I'm putting my money on the lady."

17

"Winner keeps ten percent," Fargo said.

"That's fair." It was the pudgy man Fargo had seen earlier handing out the flyers. "I'll keep track of the money. Give me your bets, men."

In a moment there were two huge piles of greenbacks and gold eagles on the gallows platform. Fargo eyed them. Ten percent of the winnings would be a nice haul for one afternoon—for either one of them. Dena caught his glance and flashed him a grin.

"You ain't got a chance," she said in a tough voice for the crowd's benefit. She tossed a penny high in the air, and Fargo slipped the Colt from his holster, brought the barrel up fast, and fired. The penny jounced against the sky, and the audience whistled and cheered—the ones with money on Fargo, anyway.

Again and again Dena and Fargo took turns tossing pennies and firing. Again and again the coins fell to earth as mangled bits of metal. They shot right-handed, left-handed, standing on one foot, looking in a mirror, lying on their backs, every which way. Ten minutes became half an hour, then an hour. When the crowd ran out of pennies, somebody was sent over to the saloon to change a few greenbacks. It was clear the match was going to be a draw or would go on all night. The crowd started to lose interest. One man stepped forward and demanded his bet back. Then another decided he'd had enough too. Fargo realized every time a man took his bet back, the game got less interesting to the ones left in it. Eventually, they would all take their money back. Something had to be done.

Dena threw a penny high in the air, and Fargo took aim, then, at the last second, shifted the barrel and fired. The penny fell straight to earth.

"Goddamn it," Fargo swore in the heavy, startled silence. "Goddamn. I can't believe I missed."

Deadeye Dena flashed him an exasperated look as if to say, I saw you miss that shot on purpose. They shook hands.

The crowd went wild, at least the ones who had won their bets. They pressed forward as the pudgy man counted out ten percent of the winnings and handed them to Dena. Fargo and Dena pushed their way out of the crowd and wandered over to where her palomino was waiting.

"That wasn't fair and square and you know it," Dena said once they were out of earshot of anybody. She jingled her pockets, heavy with the loot. "You want half?"

"Hell no," Fargo said. "You keep it. Losing was better than letting all that money get up and walk away again. Why don't you join me for some dinner?"

"Haven't you got an offer from somebody your own age?" she teased. "Nothing I like better than dining with the dashing Skye Fargo," she added. "But damn it, I promised I'd do a gig down in Cheyenne tomorrow morning. It's a big show, and there's a promoter from back east going to be there. Might be a big break." She stamped her foot in exasperation. "I'd rather have a jaw wag with you and hear all your tales. But, I'm running behind, and I've got to ride all night to get there."

"Invitation's always open," Fargo said, disappointed. Too bad. It was never dull when Deadeye Dena was around. She mounted her palomino. She was one hard-driving woman, tough as pemmican, but bighearted. He watched as she rode off and disappeared. The sun was lowering in the west, and it was just before sundown. He wondered if Mack was waiting inside the hotel.

The dilapidated lobby was furnished with shabby horsehair couches and two dead palms planted in spittoons. Behind the reception desk sat a bespectacled young clerk, his pale blond hair center parted and slicked down. He was reading a newspaper.

"I'm looking for somebody named Mack," Fargo said.

The clerk continued reading, so Fargo repeated the request a little louder. There was no response. Was the clerk deaf? Fargo reached across the counter and tapped the man on the shoulder. He nearly jumped out of his skin, and the newspaper flew everywhere.

"What do you want?" the clerk asked nervously as he gathered up the pages. Fargo repeated himself. The clerk adjusted his glasses and sat down again.

"Never heard of anybody named Mack," he said shortly. He buried his nose in the newsprint again. Fargo reached across the counter and grabbed the hotel registry. The clerk lowered his paper.

"Hey! Hey! You can't do that!"

"Just looking," Fargo said calmly, his eyes scanning the ink signatures of the hotel guests. Nope. No one with a name even close to Mack. Fargo handed the book back to the clerk, who snatched it away and returned to reading his paper.

Maybe if he sat and waited for a while, Fargo thought. Mack was sure to turn up. It was just on sunset. He settled down on one of the horsehair couches, which prickled him. He shifted around. He'd sat on rocks a whole lot softer. Why the hell did anybody make couches so damned uncomfortable? He slouched and pulled his hat brim down over his eyes. He could doze and still keep an eye out from time to time on whoever came through the lobby. The grandfather clock ticked. Nine o'clock came and went, and the lobby was still deserted. Hell's Picket was a helluva quiet town.

At half past nine Fargo heard horses pull up outside. He rose and pushed back his hat expectantly. There were several voices, two men arguing, but he couldn't make out the words. The door swung open, and a beefy black-haired man in fancy duds strode in, his jinglebobs clattering on the floor. God, how he hated jinglebobs, Fargo thought. The noisy oversized spurs made the sound of an approaching idiot. The big man wore a hat with a silver band, and his broad shoulders and muscular arms strained against the dark fabric of his jacket.

Could this be Mack? Fargo didn't like the looks of him. He started to move forward, then hesitated as a couple entered. The young man, in rancher's clothes, was gaunt and angry-looking.

Under his red hair his pale face was flushed with fury, and he darted fierce looks at the big fellow. On his arm was a young woman. Fargo's eyes ran appreciatively over her willowy form, the curves of her narrow waist and rounded hips were poured into a yellow gingham dress. Her full breasts swelled over the top of the low-cut bodice, and her curling strawberry hair fell over her shoulders to her waist. With one hand she clutched at the young man's arm, while the other nervously twisted a handkerchief. She kept her eyes on the floor.

The big man banged on the counter to get the clerk's attention.

"Yes, sir!" The clerk jumped up. "Oh, it's you, sir."

Obviously, the clerk knew the big guy. So he couldn't be Mack.

"Got my room?" the big man growled. "There's three of us."

"Certainly, sir. Room Three." The clerk handed him the key.

"Get my horses over to the livery," the big man said. He jerked his head toward the staircase, and the young man and woman started up the steps. The big man followed, then noticed Fargo for the first time. He stopped and turned, staring him down. Behind him the young woman raised her eyes, and Fargo saw them for the first time. They were sad, suffering, surrounded by dark circles. What the hell was wrong with her? he wondered. Maybe she was ill or in mourning for somebody. She noticed his gaze, and she returned it, a flicker of interest passing, and then she looked down again and leaned against the young man, who held her arm.

"What're you looking at?" the big man growled. Fargo shrugged. No use starting trouble over nothing. "Who the hell is *he*?" the big guy shot at the hotel clerk.

The clerk adjusted his spectacles and sniffed. "Just some troublemaker passing through town," the clerk said.

The big guy glowered at Fargo, then continued up the stairs. The clerk left the lobby to take care of the horses. Fargo glanced at the clock. It was quarter to ten. Whoever Mack was, he hadn't shown. Fargo paced the empty lobby a few times, then decided to stable his horse for the night and take a room in the hotel. Even though he preferred sleeping out in the open, a long hot bath and a feather bed would be a welcome change. And if Mack did show up the next morning, he'd be right here. Fargo left the hotel, unhitched his pinto, and took it down to the livery stable where he found the hotel clerk. They walked back to the hotel together, and the clerk checked him into a room.

"Room Two," the clerk said, pushing the registry book across the counter. "Sign right here." Fargo scribbled his name and read the name of the big man who had signed in just before him.

"Sam Blade," Fargo read aloud. "Is that the same Sam Blade who ran that casino across the way? The one that went out of business because rumor got around the games were fixed?"

"That's Mr. Blade," the clerk said stiffly.

"Who's the girl? And the other guy?" Fargo asked. The clerk's eyes widened with suspicion.

"None of my business," he said stiffly, picking up his newspaper.

"Yeah," said Fargo. He hoisted his saddlebag and ascended the stairs.

The room was comfortable enough, with a big brass bed that was plump and inviting. In the morning, Fargo decided, he'd call for a hot bath and have a pancake breakfast while he waited for Mack to materialize. He poured some water into the bowl on the washstand and was dashing the trail dust off his face when he heard voices through the thin wall—a woman's voice, then a man's, two men.

Normally, he didn't like messing in other people's business, but there was something in the tones that captured his attention. The woman's voice was plaintive, begging. She was in some kind of trouble. Fargo straightened up and pressed his ear to the wall. The words were muffled, but he could make them out.

" . . . please, please don't, Mr. Blade," she sobbed.

It was Sam Blade and the woman and young man he'd seen down in the lobby.

"He'll do as I say and shut up!" Blade's deep voice responded. "I've had enough of his talk. Just remember what's going to happen if you don't cooperate."

There was the sound of a crash and a thud against the wall. The young woman screamed, and a shot rang out, then another.

Fargo leapt to the door and ran into the corridor. He tried the knob of Room Three, but it was locked. Inside he could hear the woman sobbing. He gave the oak door a swift kick, but it held. Fargo drew his Colt and fired at the lock, once, twice. The metal shattered, and he kicked again. The door flew open.

Fargo held his smoking Colt before him. Sam Blade stood, pistol in hand, looking down. At his feet lay the young man, shot in the head and chest. His features were slack, eyes staring. A pool of blood was spreading across the floor. Kneeling on the carpet beside the dead youth was the woman in yellow. She turned her grief-stricken face to Fargo, then got to her feet and flung herself toward him. Fargo caught her with one hand as she collapsed against him. He circled her waist with one arm. She was breathing fast, like a scared bird.

"Drop the gun," Fargo said to Blade.

Sam Blade glanced up and seemed to notice him for the first time. He shook his head as if to clear it, then slowly glanced at Fargo's Colt. For a long minute he stared at his own gun. Then he smiled. It was an ugly smile.

Behind him Fargo could hear the pounding of feet on the stairs and voices calling out. Somebody came to the open doorway and gasped. It was the clerk, who took one look at the dead man on the floor and retreated.

"Murder! Murder!" the clerk shouted as he ran back down the stairs.

"I said drop it," Fargo repeated. "I'm not asking again."

Sam Blade shifted the barrel of his gun and aimed it at the woman in Fargo's arm. His black eyes glittered, never leaving Fargo's.

"Shoot me, and my last act's going to be to pull this trigger. The bullet will rip right through her pretty flesh."

He was one cool customer, Fargo thought. Most men would have panicked, but Sam Blade knew just what card to play next. Fargo thought fast. If he pushed her off to the right and dove in the opposite direction, Sam might shoot and miss. Or he might not miss. If he fired at Sam's gun, he might throw off the shot. But maybe not. If he pushed her behind him, he could take the bullet himself. Fargo had just decided to do that when he heard the approach of heavy footsteps.

Sheriff Sikes appeared in the doorway. The bespectacled clerk peered around the corner behind him.

"What the hell?" Sikes exclaimed, spotting the dead man. "Sam Blade! What's going on here?"

"Unhand the girl," Sam Blade growled, motioning with his pistol toward Fargo. She was trembling in his arm.

"The hell I will!" Fargo said. "Drop *your* gun!"

In the doorway Sheriff Sikes drew his pistol. "Both of you drop 'em right now!" he barked. Sam Blade gave a smirk and threw his pistol onto the floor. Fargo followed suit. The woman sagged against him, and Fargo steered her toward a chair. She sat, then buried her face in her hands. "Now, what's going on here?" the sheriff asked. "Blade, what are you doing back in town?"

"Just came in tonight to do some business," Blade said. "I went downstairs to fetch some . . . more water, and I heard some shots. I came running back to find this . . . this bandit murdered Scotty MacKenzie!"

Sheriff Sikes glanced at Fargo and shifted the barrel of his pistol to cover him.

"That's not what happened," Fargo said.

"Step away from the girl," Sikes warned.

"Sure," Fargo said, moving away. "But that's not what happened. I was next door in my room when I heard them in here arguing. Next thing, I heard two shots, and I came to find out what happened. The door was locked, so I shot the lock. Sam Blade's the one who killed him. Ask her," Fargo finished, gesturing toward the woman in yellow. "She was a witness."

"Well?" Sikes asked her. "What do you say, miss? What's your name?"

The young woman looked up, her tear-streaked face twisted with pain. "Julie," she said softly. "Julie MacKenzie."

She glanced at the dead man on the floor, then at Fargo. She opened her mouth to speak. Sam Blade cleared his throat loudly. Julie looked at Blade for a long moment, turned bright red, and looked down at the floor.

"He did it," Julie said quietly. "He killed my brother."

"Who did it?" the sheriff asked, his voice short. "Sam Blade?" She shook her head no, her face hidden by her hair. "Then this other fellow, Skye Fargo? He did it?" There was a long pause, and she nodded yes, but would not look up.

"She's lying," Fargo said. "I don't know why, but she's covering up for Sam Blade." Blade's black eyes were hard as steel.

"That's *your* story," Sheriff Sikes said, looking at him suspiciously. "This your gun?" He picked up Fargo's Colt and sniffed it. He opened the chamber and looked inside. "Two bullets missing." Sikes walked over to the body and toed it. "One to the head, one to the chest."

"I shot the lock, remember?" Fargo said. "Besides, I didn't even know this man, Scotty MacKenzie."

"But earlier he was asking all kinds of questions," the clerk put in, nervously combing his hair with his fingers. "Downstairs, when he checked in—real curious questions."

"The hell I did!" Fargo shot back. "I just asked who they were. That doesn't prove anything."

"Proves you were interested," the sheriff said mildly, sticking Fargo's Colt into his belt. A couple of deputies appeared in the doorway, breathing hard, guns in hand.

"It proves nothing," Fargo repeated, exasperated. "Look, Sheriff, you told me yourself this afternoon, a man's not guilty until proven. Can't you see Julie MacKenzie is scared of Sam Blade? She's covering up for something, and I'm the fall guy."

"That's a good story, Mr. Fargo," Sikes said. "But the way I see it, I got a murder and two witnesses. Looks pretty clear to me. We'll get you in front of the judge first thing in the morning. Come on, boys."

The two deputies stepped into the room, and one pulled out handcuffs. Sam Blade smiled. Julie refused to look up from the floor. For a moment Fargo considered running. But he knew it would only make things worse. He'd be a hunted man until he could prove himself innocent. He glanced at her. She knew the truth. And somehow, he felt that she wouldn't let an innocent man go to the gallows. He could see that in her face. No. Once out of sight of Sam Blade, she'd do some thinking, and when the judge questioned her, she'd come around. The truth would out. Fargo held his hands out in front of him while the handcuffs were put on.

"I'm sure this is going to get cleared up in front of the judge," Fargo said. "Julie MacKenzie knows I'm innocent. And besides, what kind of motive would I have to bust in here and shoot a stranger?"

Sikes gave a short laugh.

"Well, Mr. Fargo, the whole town heard your motive this very afternoon," he said. Fargo shook his head, puzzled, trying to imagine what the sheriff was talking about. "Everybody in town heard you when you jumped up and challenged that lady shootist. She said, 'What are you doing in town?' and you said, 'I'm looking for something to shoot at.'"

Two of the deputies exchanged knowing looks and nodded. Fargo felt stunned. Sheriff Sikes jammed the barrel of his pistol in Fargo's back as they moved toward the door.

"I heard you, Fargo," Sikes said. "And I thought to myself that I'd better keep an eye on you. Well, you found something to shoot at after all. But we got you now. This is a law-abiding town, Mr. Fargo. And we don't welcome your kind."

Fargo's thoughts whirled as he neared the doorway. He glanced back at Julie. She sat as if paralyzed, refusing to meet his gaze. It all depended on her now.

"Thank you, Sheriff Sikes," Sam Blade called after them. "I always said Hell's Picket was a fine town."

Fargo spent the night pacing the small cell of the jail. For a couple of hours he thought of escape. They hadn't found the throwing knife strapped to his ankle, but it was no use. The bars were thick, and the double guards were wary. At dawn they passed him a cup of coffee and a roll very carefully through the bars of the door.

Then six armed men arrived to escort him to the trial. There was no possibility of escape. For the next few hours Fargo felt as if he were moving through a bad dream. The trial was a joke, a farce. The circuit judge, who clearly had a hangover, sat behind the sheriff's desk. Sam Blade appeared with Julie MacKenzie on his arm, and once again she refused to look at him, answering the questions put to her by Sheriff Sikes and the judge in a quiet voice or with the nod of her head. And Sam Blade had his story down pat, details and all. At the end Fargo knew he'd lost, and when the gavel came down, the judge got to his feet.

"Guilty of the shooting murder of Scotty MacKenzie," the judge said, swaying slightly. He hiccuped. "I charge Mr. . . . he looked down at the papers on the desk before him . . . Mr. Skye Fargo to be hanged by the neck until dead."

There was a muffled cry, and Fargo saw Julie MacKenzie start to rise to her feet. Then she went white, stumbled, and slumped down in her chair. She had fainted. Sam Blade put his big arm around her and half carried her out of the room.

The six men closed in on Fargo and hustled him outside. Justice had not been done after all. Now he would have to find a method of escape so he could prove his innocence another way, outside the law. But escape how? His hands were still cuffed, and the six men surrounded him—all armed, all careful. The late morning sun blazed down. He was marched through the dusty streets as the citizens of Hell's Picket pointed at him and muttered to one another.

"Murderer!" one of the women shouted.

"Hangin's too good for a murderer!" a man put in.

With a sense of unreality Fargo wondered where the six men were taking him. Then with a cold chill he saw that they were heading straight toward the main square. Surely, they were not taking him directly from the trial to the gallows? But with every step, reality became clearer.

The tall wooden platform came into view, surrounded by the false fronts of the old hotel, Sam

Blade's gaudy casino, and the windowed shops. The sun beat down, and he could hear the grains of dust grinding beneath his boots with every step. The man next to him held a pistol in his left hand. Fargo realized if he could swing around and grab for the gun with his cuffed hands, he could hold them off, run for a horse, and make his escape. It was a long shot, but now it was his only shot.

Fargo faked a stumble, brought up both hands, and clubbed the man to his left, who went down, groaning. He swung right, his cuffed hands before him, and caught the second man with a jaw-shattering arc. He kicked out, and a third man went down, holding his groin. Fargo clutched at the man's weapon and felt the warm metal of the gun in his grip just as a heavy blow fell across the back of his neck. Stars exploded in the white hot sky, and he felt himself going down.

The heat beneath his body woke him up. Sweat trickled down his face and into his ears. A fly buzzed. There was a heavy drumbeat in his head. The heat rose around him. It was blasting hot. Where the hell was he?

"I'll give you a hundred," a man called out.

"Why this hayburner's worth more than that!" another voice said. "And there's a gun and saddle to go with it!"

"Hundred fifty."

"Two hundred."

"Two ten."

"Sold!"

Fargo forced open his eyes. He lay in the noon sunlight on the gallows platform. The square was filled with people. They were gathered around a black-and-white pinto—his Ovaro. Another man came to lead the horse away. As he took its bridle, it balked and resisted.

"A good horse whip'll cure that temper," a man shouted. The crowd laughed.

"He's awake!" someone said.

Immediately, the crowd turned toward him, and rough hands pulled at him, helping him to his feet. Fargo realized that the noose was already around his neck. The sheriff stood on the platform with his men.

"We had to take this little knife off you, Mr. Fargo," the sheriff said, swinging the throwing knife in front of his eyes. Obviously, they had searched him more carefully while he'd been unconscious. "And we wanted to wait until you woke up, Mr. Fargo," Sheriff Sikes said. "It ain't sporting to hang somebody who's asleep. You got any last words?"

Fargo realized the end of the trail had finally come. He felt the cool breeze against his sweaty face, the warmth of the sun on his shoulders. Many a time over the years, he'd faced down death and won. But now death finally got the upper hand. In the square before him was his horse, the loyal Ovaro. Now it belonged to somebody else. He caught a flash of yellow on the front porch of the hotel. Sam Blade and Julie MacKenzie stood there, ready to watch his execution. She knew she was sending an innocent men to his death, and yet she didn't speak up. Why? What was the power that Sam Blade had over her? Now he'd never know. All that was left for him to do was to die like a man.

"Any last words?" the sheriff said impatiently. Fargo heard the creak of the trapdoor below him. And he knew it was moments before they pulled the lever and he would drop into space. If he was lucky, his neck would break and the end would be quick.

"Yeah," Fargo said loudly. His eyes were on the figure in yellow on the hotel porch. "I'm an innocent man. Sam Blade killed Scotty MacKenzie. You're hanging the wrong man."

In the silence Fargo waited for her to call out—to tell the truth—but she never spoke. Instead, the figure of Julie MacKenzie standing on the hotel porch twisted her head away, not looking toward him.

Sheriff Sikes nodded to one of his men. Fargo heard the rusty creak of the trapdoor mechanism and felt the boards give way beneath him. As if in slow motion, he felt gravity lay its hands on him and pull him downward into space, felt himself dropping, down, down, the thick, rough rope around his neck, down. Nothing could save him now.

2

Fargo was falling through space. The roar of the crowded square was a distant hum in his ears and a bright blur before his eyes. The beating of his heart was deafening. His thoughts came clear in his last moments of life. No regrets, except the senseless waste of dying because of a man like Sam Blade. In a second the end would come, a sudden tightening of the noose would catch the full force of his falling weight to snap his neck and end his life . . . falling . . .

A pop sounded far away, then another, like a string of firecrackers. Fargo felt a slackness he could not identify, a quickening of something as he fell. Then he hit hard on the earth, his legs giving way beneath him, and he sprawled in the dust. The snaking rope fell on top of him.

The rope had snapped, he thought at first. He'd landed underneath the gallows. He leapt to his feet, yanking the noose from around his neck. There was a deathly silence around him, and the disbelieving crowd stood paralyzed. Then Fargo heard the popping sound again and, as if through a fog, caught sight of a familiar figure on a palomino, pistols in the air—Deadeye Dena. She'd shot the hanging rope clean through. She must have gotten word somehow that he was in trouble and circled back to Hell's Picket.

Fargo's vision and thoughts cleared. He was alive, goddamn it. They hadn't killed him yet. The rage at the injustice rose in him like the molten fire of a volcano. Not far from him was the gleaming white-and-black Ovaro. A slack-jawed man held its reins and stared at him in disbelief as if he were a ghost.

The crowd suddenly came to life. Men drew their pistols and shouted. Women shrieked. Fargo made a dash from under the gallows platform. He shoved men aside and leapt onto the back of the pinto as the first bullets flew through the air. Hell, if he got out of this, it would be a miracle. A rain of bullets whizzed by him from the direction of the gallows. Meanwhile, from the edge of the crowd, Dena seemed to be keeping up a pretty steady fire.

Fargo ducked low in the saddle. He pulled the pinto around in the panicked crowd, which scattered to get away from the gunfire. The Ovaro reared, then plunged forward, nostrils flaring. His holster had been slung over the saddle, and Fargo drew his Colt and turned about in the saddle, toward the gallows. On the platform Sheriff Sikes knelt, holding his arm, as did several other deputies. One was awkwardly trying to shoot left-handed. Others lay groaning on the platform. The one upright deputy took aim at him, but before Fargo could pull the trigger, the pop of gunfire from Dena's direction exploded again. The deputy screamed, dropped his pistol, and grabbed his right elbow in agony. Even in the middle of a desperate battle, Dena was using her head, Fargo realized in a flash. She could have plugged every one of those men straight between the eyes. Instead, she was winging them all, one by one. Murdering a bunch of lawmen wasn't the point. Getting away was.

Fargo ducked another bullet that came whining over his head and saw the hotel porch coming up fast on his left. At the railing stood Julie MacKenzie, her pretty face twisted with a mix of relief and terror. She was the one person who could get him out of this mess, he realized. The one person who had seen Sam Blade shoot Scottie MacKenzie. Beside her, Sam Blade raised his silver derringer, and Fargo was suddenly staring into its small black barrel. Fargo brought his colt up in a smooth motion, fired, and heard the simultaneous retort from Blade's gun. Fargo hunched down as the bullet shrieked by.

Fargo leaned out as he passed the porch and made a grab for Julie, catching hold of her around the waist before she could pull away. He pulled her up onto the saddle, throwing her in front of him like a sack of flour, as she screamed in fright and struggled in his grasp.

Fargo urged the pinto forward, and it sped up the street in a cloud of dust as bullets flew overhead. Behind him came the sound of pounding hooves, and Fargo saw Deadeye Dena riding hell-bent after him. Beyond her in the dusty street, men were running about like angry ants, some firing their guns, others untethering horses. There'd be a posse on their trail in a matter of moments. The sturdy black-and-white pinto galloped like lightning, and the last wooden buildings of Hell's Picket flashed by. Then they were out on the open trail heading toward the low hills to the east that ascended like a series of steps. From the top they could strike out into the wild country, hole up for a while, then figure out what to do next. Fargo glanced back again to see Dena on the palomino falling behind only a little as they neared the brush-dense hills. There wasn't a horse in the West that could keep up with the Ovaro, but Fargo was glad to see Dena's palomino was damned fast. They'd need every second of speed.

They gained the top of the first rise, and Fargo glanced back at the little town of Hell's Picket. No posse yet. Since most of the deputies had been winged by Dena, they were probably still organizing the men. But they'd be along. Fargo pushed on, driving the horses full out, galloping hard. Julie MacKenzie was getting bounced around hard on the saddle horn as she lay in front of him. No time to stop yet. They couldn't keep this up for long, but he wanted to gain the top of the highest rise before they paused to let the horses take a breather.

When they surmounted the last hill and had a view of the land all around them, Fargo pulled up, and a cloud of dust engulfed them. The Ovaro was breathing hard, its ribs like bellows, and a fine fleck of hot foam glistened on its black-and-white coat. Hell's Picket lay five miles behind, a dark spot on the sage plain in the distance. As Fargo watched, he saw a dust plume rise from the edge of town. That would be the posse setting out.

"Okay, let's get you settled," Fargo said to Julie. "That's not the most comfortable way to ride, and we've got a hard pull ahead of us." He gripped her slender waist to help her, and suddenly she struggled in his grasp, clawing him with her nails and trying to bite him as he held her.

"Hold on there," Fargo said as she threatened to slip off the horse. Dena pulled up beside them.

"You got some girl troubles, Fargo?" Dena snapped. "Settle down, miss. We ain't got time for this."

"Let me go!" Julie cried, trying to wrench free. Her curly strawberry hair was a wild tangled mass, and her blue eyes were cold with anger. "You two bandits got out of town just fine. Now let me go!"

"Nothing doing," Fargo shot back, pinioning her arms behind her and holding her from sliding down the side of the pinto. He pulled her leg over the horse and held her upright, hard against him. "Hold still!" he commanded, speaking into her ear. Her heart was beating like a bird's. "Listen up, Julie MacKenzie. You're the one person who knows I didn't shoot your brother. And you lied to cover up for Sam Blade. Why is beyond me. But I'm going to find out. Meanwhile, you hold still or else."

He felt her weaken and then slump forward. He loosened his grip on her, and immediately she pitched to one side in an attempt to jump down.

Fargo was ready this time. His Colt was still in his hand, and he spun it about on his finger so he was gripping the barrel. He cold-cocked her with a light tap. She collapsed against him. That would keep her quiet a few hours, but she'd wake up with a helluva headache. He propped her limp body against him, pulled his gun belt out from underneath her, and strapped it on, holstering his gun.

"You're rough on your women, Fargo," Dena said, a grin on her leathery face. Her palomino was foaming with sweat, its nostrils flared. They needed a few minutes more to let the horses catch their wind after the hard pull up the hills. "Which way now?"

Fargo eyed the open land spread out beneath the white sky of midday summer. Wyoming Territory was big country. To the east, endless mesas, buttes, and dry grasslands filled with buffalo. Farther south, the Oregon Trail, jammed with wagons of homesteaders heading west. Directly west, the jagged impassable mountains of the Salt River Range.

"North," Fargo decided, thinking of the folded hills, the deep sheltering pine forests, the twisting rivers and canyons that could hide a man forever. "We'll head north into Wind River country, then angle westward up to the Old Gap lands. We can lose 'em there." Dena nodded agreement. "You lead," Fargo said. "I'll cover our rear."

"We'll make better time if your pinto's setting the pace," Dena pointed out. She patted the neck of her palomino. "Trusty's got his pride. He'll pull hard to keep up with any old Ovaro."

"And pull too hard," Fargo said. "When your horse goes short or lame, we'll be up shit creek. You lead—your pace."

"I see your point, Fargo," Dena said. "North it is."

The palomino started forward, and the Ovaro swung into line behind. Fargo held Julie MacKenzie's slumped form against him, one arm around her small waist. Her fine hair blew in the wind and tickled his face. It glistened red-gold in the harsh sun, which beat down on her pale skin. Her full breasts swelled over the top of her neckline. She had a lot of spirit, trying to get away like that. Fargo wondered again what her story was. Why would she come to the defense of the man who had shot her brother in cold blood right in front of her eyes? He puzzled over everything he had seen at the hotel the night before, recalling her words, remembering the young Scottie MacKenzie lying dead on the floor. And the tall, dark figure of Sam Blade—at the thought of him, Fargo felt his fists tighten on the reins until his knuckles grew white.

They rode through the long afternoon, driving farther north, not bothering to hide their tracks. Speed was what counted now. They paused only to rest and to water the horses. Both were doing well, the Ovaro spirited and fresh. The palomino showed some signs of weariness, but was holding up. Several times Fargo caught sight of dust on the trail behind them. He calculated they'd gained a good ten miles lead on the posse. It wasn't much out here in the open country. But once they reached the convoluted hills of the Old Gap country, they could throw the posse off their trail. Then that ten miles might as well be a thousand. The posse could wander around in the dense forests, black canyons, and dead-end valleys for months and never find them. And the posse knew it too. They were undoubtedly riding top speed, trying to catch them in the open country.

The sun was a red globe sinking beyond the distant peaks when they reached the pine-clad hills. As the light faded to dusk, they cantered along a dim game trail that led upward between the hills. Fargo's eyes adjusted to the gathering darkness beneath the trees, and he took the lead. As it grew darker, they slowed to a walk, picking their way along and letting the Ovaro find its sure footing. Julie came awake with a groan, then gasped as she remembered what had happened.

"Keep still or I'll put you out again," Fargo growled. She remained sullen and quiet, but he knew she'd try to escape again until he could talk some sense into her. The rising moon blinked among the tall pine trees, and Fargo was grateful for the dim light. It would help him for what would come next.

They came to a wide mountain stream glittering silver in the moonlight. An owl hooted in the black forest. Fargo's keen ears picked up the faint flutter of its sudden flight and the squeak of a feckless chipmunk or rat caught in its talons. He called a halt and dismounted, lifting Julie down. The horses drank, and Fargo dashed the ice-cold glacier water over his face and neck. The nights were cool at this altitude. Julie, hunched down beside the stream, was shivering. Fargo fetched his buckskin jacket from the saddlebag and tossed it to her. She looked up in surprise. He pulled on a flannel shirt and leather vest.

"Keep an eye on her," he said to Dena. The spot couldn't have been more perfect, he thought, as he bent to examine the tracks in the moist earth with his sensitive fingertips. Lots of game tracks here, fresh ones, easy to read where the moonlight fell between the tall trees. Across the stream the dim trail continued on between the low humps of two hills. Downstream he spotted a rocky bank that led to a large slope of scree, washed by the moonlight and bordered by black forest on all sides. Anybody trying to throw somebody off the trail would ride into the stream and then emerge on the rocks and head off in another direction. Sheriff Sikes was no fool. That's exactly what he and his posse would figure.

Fargo returned to the crossing. Julie sat on a rock, hunched in Fargo's buckskin jacket. She had taken off her boots and was dipping her white feet gingerly into the cold stream water. Dena was cleaning her pistol.

"They'll be through here in half an hour or so," Fargo said. "Let's get a move on. It's time to throw them off our trail."

Julie shot him a startled look, then stood reluctantly, dried her feet on her skirt, and pulled on her boots. She left them unlaced as she hobbled toward the horse. She shivered again.

"Doesn't help to stick your feet in ice water," Fargo commented as he held the Ovaro for her to mount.

"My shoes are tight," she mumbled.

He swung up behind her, enjoying the feel of her pillowy rear pressing against him, the willowy form of her between his arms. If only she weren't so much damn trouble, he thought.

Fargo turned the Ovaro upstream along the soggy bank for about ten paces, then plunged into the stream. Dena followed. Once in the water, he pulled the horse about and let it pick its slow way downstream through the rushing water.

"You . . . you must be hiding our tracks," Julie said.

"Mmm," Fargo said, preoccupied, his eyes on the rocky bank coming closer. The Ovaro crossed nearer to the rocks, and Fargo angled the pinto so that it left one clear hoofprint in a small muddy patch right by the rocks. As the pinto scrambled out of the stream onto the rocks, Fargo dismounted and led it along the rocky rim of the scree. The surefooted horse moved slowly forward on the loose rocks as the palomino came behind.

"You're doing this so they won't see our tracks on the rocks," Julie said. She seemed to be watching everything he did with great interest. Fargo didn't answer her. They had gone maybe a hundred yards along the rocky shore when he spotted a large flat rock half submerged in the stream with the water running over it. He led the Ovaro to it and back into the stream. There would be no track there to show where they had gone.

"Where . . . where are we going now?" Julie asked nervously.

Fargo ignored her and pulled the Ovaro around to head upstream again, past the slope of scree to the trail crossing. Just to one side of the trail, he motioned to Dena to lead as he brought the Ovaro out on the far bank. He heard a small splash in the stream and wondered why trout would be jumping at this hour. He kept to one side of the trail, winding back and forth between the thick pines, keeping to the dense thatch of pine needles on the forest floor. Meanwhile, Julie sat stiff as a board, watching everything. When they reached a curve in the trail, Fargo halted again and handed the reins of the pinto to Dena.

"Where are you going?" Julie asked nervously. "I bet they're right behind us." Fargo ignored her completely. One minute she was trying to get away from him, and now she seemed to be concerned that the sheriff would catch up.

He retraced their trail carefully in the moonlight, glad to see there were scarcely any hoofprints on the thick mat of the pine-needled forest floor. Where there were, he scattered extra needles to hide the telltale signs of their passage. He reached the bank of the stream where they had left deep-scored prints in the mud. He was about to obscure the tracks when the black shape of something lying on the bank caught his eye. He picked up Julie's boot, which lay half in the water.

"Little bitch," he muttered. That's what he had heard splash in the stream. She was trying to leave a sign for their pursuers as to which direction they had gone. He set his anger aside for the moment and scooped water into his hat, pouring it over the bank until the traces of prints disappeared in the mud. Just as he finished, he heard the sounds of horses some distance away. He'd used up their slim advantage by setting up this diversion. If it worked, they'd gain a full day, maybe more. If it didn't . . .

Fargo refused to consider that possibility as he quickly retraced his steps, gripping Julie's boot in his hand. When he came up, Julie had drawn her feet up under her skirt. Fargo pulled her down off the horse. Julie cried out as Fargo lifted her skirt and Dena gasped in surprise. Both her feet were bare. Fargo gripped her tight against him and squeezed the breath out of her.

"This is no game we're playing," Fargo hissed in her ear. "They catch up to me and I'm a dead man. And Dena will swing too just for saving me. I'm not going to let that happen. Now. I found this down on the bank where the trail leaves the stream. Where's the other one?"

Julie hesitated a moment, and Fargo squeezed her again. Hell, he hated to scare the girl, but it seemed to be the only way to make her cooperate.

"On . . . on the . . . rocks," Julie said, a sob in her voice. He knew what she meant. On the scree slope.

"That's good," Dena said with a barking laugh. "Let's go, Trailsman."

Fargo smiled as he loosed the bandanna from his neck and used it to gag Julie. Perfect, he thought as he helped her back up onto the pinto and used a short piece of rawhide thong to tie her wrists together behind her. He stowed her one boot in his saddlebag. It was just as well she was barefoot. That might make her think twice if she was tempted to run away.

As he mounted and they picked their way slowly through the pine forest, he thought of the stream crossing they left behind. Yes, perfect. The posse would arrive. First they'd see the tangle of prints where they had dismounted to drink. Then hoof-prints that led for a little way upstream and plunged in. That would make them think that Fargo was trying to lead them in the wrong direction. And they would concentrate their search downstream. There they would find the slope of scree, one seemingly accidental hoofprint in a patch of mud, and Julie's boot left as a cry for help. Sheriff Sikes, Sam Blade, and the posse would be chasing their tails in the wrong direction for the better part of the night and a day at least. They'd search the banks of the stream and the border of the scree slope for the rest of the trail.

Fargo slowed the pace through the long night to give the horses a needed rest. They moved at a steady pace as the cold moon climbed overhead and then descended and disappeared in the west. The night wind made the pines whistle eerily. Julie dozed, her head dropped forward. Her sleep was disturbed by bad dreams, and she twitched and mumbled in her sleep. Dena glanced over from time to time as Julie cried out.

"No, not Pa. No. Please," Julie muttered at one

point. "Please don't. Ma, oh, Ma." Then she was quiet again.

"She's sure got a pile of trouble," Dena said quietly.

"And she *is* a pile of trouble," Fargo answered. They were heading northwest, walking the horses side by side across a high, open meadow surrounded by tall firs. The sky to the east brightened, and the birds were rioting in the brush, their sounds a cascade of trills and melodies.

"I haven't had time to thank you for saving my life," Fargo said. "You missed your big chance in Cheyenne with that East Coast promoter."

"Don't mention it," Dena replied with a shrug. "You'd do the same for me. Anyway, I'd probably dry up like an old buzzard if I found myself east of the Mississippi."

"How'd you hear about the hanging?"

"I was halfway to Cheyenne when I stopped at a little town called Altitude to get some grub for breakfast. It was damned lucky too, because the only eating place in town also had the telegraph office. And somebody from Hell's Picket was passing on the gossip about you doing some murder. Well, I didn't wait to get the whole story. I just hightailed it back. And damn it, if I'd been three minutes later, I'd have come for your funeral. So, what in hell happened?"

Fargo recounted the story about Sam Blade and the murder in the hotel room.

"What I don't understand," Fargo said, "is how she could stand by and see an innocent man hanged. She'd have to live with that for the rest of her life."

"Maybe the alternative is worse," Dena said thoughtfully after a moment.

"Maybe," Fargo said. He'd find out when they camped, he decided. They needed a day now to rest up and let the horses regain their strength. As the sun rose, Fargo looked around for a suitably secure place. They reentered the forest and wound their way up a steep, dim trail, crossing countless streams, deep in the back country and far from any settlements. Finally, they came to a broad lake lying in the arms of a tall peak. At one end a deep cleft led to a notch in the mountain, and below it was an outcropping of tall rocks.

Fargo headed toward them and found the perfect campsite, surrounded on all sides by the rocks, which would hide the light of their fire. Wind speeding across the lake would help dispel the rising smoke. Unless somebody accidentally stumbled on top of them, they would be safe here for a while.

While Dena unpacked supplies, Fargo untied Julie's gag and rawhide thong. Her eyes were dark-ringed and troubled, and she seemed completely subdued. But Fargo knew he'd have to keep a sharp lookout. Exhausted and silent, the three of them drank water from the clear lake and chewed on some pemmican and dried berries. Dena motioned Julie to lie down on the bedroll, then tied one end of the rawhide thong to her wrist and made it fast to her own. She lay down herself in a nest of Indian blankets, her pistol close at hand. Fargo left them to scout out the lake.

Three hours later, he returned, having walked the perimeter of the lake. This was rich country. He had put some fishing lines into the water and already caught three rainbow trout. And there were rabbit runs crisscrossing the brush, so he set snares not far from camp. The marsh at the mouth of the lake was choked with wild onions and various herbs, and he'd brought a bundle of those too. And he'd spotted a hollow stump with buzzing bees where they could collect some wild honey. Best of all, there was no sign of another human being anywhere around.

Julie and Dena awoke as he walked into camp. Dena left to gather firewood. The exhaustion was hitting him now. He needed a good sleep, but first he wanted a good hot meal and, more than that, answers from Julie. She sat on a rock near the lake, gutting the trout, her bare feet in the water. There was an uncomfortable silence between them.

Fargo stripped off his vest and shirt and poured cold lake water over his hard-muscled chest and arms. He knelt down and dashed some over his face and neck as well. He glanced up to catch Julie's gaze as she admired his powerful body. Instead of the angry words he'd intended, he found himself wanting to tease her.

"Never seen a half-naked man before?" he said with a grin.

"Sure," she retorted, blushing. She smiled,

fleetingly, for the first time since he'd met her. "I've got two . . . one brother."

Her head fell forward, her wild mass of strawberry hair hiding her face. He saw her tears fall onto the trout as she worked over them, and he knew she was thinking of Scotty. He went to dry off and help Dena light the fire.

An hour later, the three of them were lounging around the fire. There had been more pan-fried trout with wild onions and dill than the three of them could eat. Fargo had made a pot of coffee, and he offered a cup to Dena, then one to Julie.

"You . . . you don't act like an outlaw," she said, taking the tin cup from his hands.

"An *outlaw*?" Dena said with a laugh. "Haven't you ever heard of Skye Fargo?"

"Just the name," Julie said with a shrug, not meeting his eyes, but speaking to Dena. "I guess he's a famous outlaw. Mr. Blade told me he'd killed hundreds of men."

"Guess I have," Fargo said. "Men who needed killing. What else did Sam Blade tell you?" Julie's gaze flicked up at him and down again.

"That you're a wanted man. You've broken the law everywhere, but they could never catch you. And about . . . what you've done . . . to women."

"Now *that's* a story I'd like to hear," Dena cackled, raising her tin cup in a toast to Fargo. "To Skye Fargo, famous Trailsman, the best love-'em-good and leave-'em-happy wild man in the Wild West." She laughed again and drank her coffee down. Julie looked puzzled.

"So that's why you were willing to let me hang instead of Sam Blade," Fargo said. "Because you believed I *deserved* hanging?" Julie shook her head yes, but her blue eyes were stormy. There was more, he knew.

"He . . . he . . ." Julie's chin trembled. "That night in the hotel, when you burst in like that, well, I just went along with his story. And later, when I found out they were going to hang you, he told me all about you—well, that you were an outlaw anyway. And then he threatened me. Said, if I didn't, he . . ."

Julie dissolved into tears, the sobs racking her. Dena shook her head and went to sit beside the girl. She put her arm around her, and Julie cried all the harder. When she regained her composure, she wiped her face on her sleeve.

"He said he'd what?" Fargo asked.

"Kill . . . kill my ma and my sister and brother," Julie said, forcing the words out. "He said if I told anybody, he'd find out and kill 'em anyway." Dena patted her on the shoulder.

"He's holding your family *hostage*?" Fargo asked. Julie nodded, as if afraid to use her voice to tell him, terror in her eyes. "Why don't you start from the beginning?"

"Mr. Blade came to our ranch about a month ago," she said.

"Where is that?" Fargo asked.

"On a bend of the Hoback River," Julie said.

"Just west of here," Dena said.

"Mr. Blade claimed my father owed him the ranch. He had a piece of paper with Pa's signature on it. Something about a card game."

"Is your pa a gambler?" Dena put in.

"Sometimes he went to town and played," Julie said. "At least I think so, because Ma never liked his going to town without her. Anyhow, Pa said fine, take the ranch, but the cattle herd is still ours. Mr. Blade got mad about that. But he said he'd let us stay for a while until we could make the money to pay him for the ranch. Only he was running things." Julie's voice choked at the memory.

"Go on," Fargo said.

"He was real mean to my brothers, Scotty and Jimmy. He beat 'em with a horsewhip. And to my little sister too. He was always . . . always putting his hands on Ma. Pa didn't like that, and a couple of days ago he had a big fight with Mr. Blade. They were yelling and screaming something terrible. Pa said he was going into town to meet somebody and get something out of the safe in the bank. And pretty soon he'd have more money than he knew what to do with, and he'd pay off Sam Blade once and for all. Mr. Blade just laughed at him. And then the next day"—she swallowed hard and wiped her tears away again—"the next day Pa fell out of the hayloft and broke his neck."

"Or was pushed," Fargo said with a question tugging at him.

"That's what Ma said," Julie continued. "Anyway, then he took me and Scotty into Hell's Picket. He forced Scotty to go to the bank and get something. They never told me what. And he made Scotty sign a paper giving him rights to our cattle. Five days from now that agreement takes effect. He's going to own everything, and we'll be flat broke. And Blade insisted he'd make us stay and work for him. But Scotty said we were just going to move out and start over. Mr. Blade said he didn't fancy working a ranch and he'd make us. That's when he and Scotty had that big fight in the hotel."

"And that's when I came in," Fargo said. "Just one thing I don't understand. Why didn't you tell the sheriff all about Sam Blade? He couldn't very well kill your family if he was in jail."

"Mr. Blade said if I told anybody—he'd send word to his men to kill everybody."

"His men?" Fargo repeated. "Men back at the ranch? How many?"

She counted on her fingers. "Ten," she said. "Maybe more. And a little guy, an Indian, but he doesn't show up very often. The rest of them are big guys. Real mean."

Fargo sat and thought. Yes, it all made sense now. But some piece of the story was bothering him. He thought it through again, the part about her father heading into Hell's Picket to meet someone. Then all the pieces fell into place, and he asked the question that had been tugging at him.

"Your father's nickname was Mack, wasn't it?" Fargo asked her.

"How'd you know that?" Julie asked.

"Because I'm the man he was supposed to meet in Hell's Picket on July first," Fargo answered. He fished the crumpled message out of his pocket and handed it to her. Julie MacKenzie read the note and cried again. This time Fargo heard more than grieving and fear in her sobs. He also heard relief, and he knew Julie trusted him now.

Fargo got to his feet and motioned to Dena. They walked a short distance away and stood by the shore.

"That was quite a story," Dena said, shaking her head. "So what's left of her family's being held hostage at the ranch." Her eyes narrowed as she looked around at the peaks sheltering the lake. "The ranch ain't far from here. Day's ride."

"This used to be Shoshoni land, didn't it?" Fargo asked her.

Dena's eyes looked faraway into the past.

"Yes," she said at last. "The last of my people lived here—until ten years ago. That was when those wagons started coming through the Old Gap. And then the gold rush out west sent that shipment through my people's land and caused my tribe so much trouble."

"A gold shipment?" Fargo asked.

"Yes," Dena said. "I heard about it from the last of my tribe who escaped the massacre. Men with wagons came through Shoshoni land. Then they disappeared. Afterward the Army came and killed the whole village. They were trying to find gold, but my people had no gold." She sighed, as if shaking off the memory. "I'll stand watch for a few hours while you get some sleep," she added briskly.

Julie was still sitting where he'd left her. Fargo lay down on his bedroll in the shade of an over-hanging rock. He'd missed two nights' sleep, one pacing in the jail cell in Hell's Picket and one in the saddle. His mind and body were exhausted almost beyond endurance. But as he lay there, his thoughts whirled. MacKenzie's note had said *This thing's got too big for me and my boys to handle.* That he could understand. Sam Blade and his men needed clearing out, and MacKenzie and his two sons couldn't handle the job all alone. But MacKenzie had also written that he was going to be *able to pay you well.* What was in the bank safe? It couldn't have been money or else he'd have paid off Sam Blade. MacKenzie had said he'd soon have more money than he knew what to do with. Was that just the loose talk of an unlucky part-time gambler? Or was there some secret here?

Fargo felt the dark hands of sleep reach up and pull him downward; then there was someone's presence near him. He opened his eyes. Julie MacKenzie was kneeling beside him, her strawberry hair an unruly halo around her face.

"I'm sorry," she said. "I'm so sorry I misjudged you." She bent over and kissed him lightly on the cheek and then got up hastily and began picking up the tin plates from around the campfire. Fargo turned on his side and let himself fall asleep.

When he awoke in late afternoon, he was alone. The fire pit was cold, Dena's blankets neatly rolled and stowed with the supplies, the clean tin utensils left to dry on a rock. Fargo rose and stretched. He spotted Dena and Julie sitting beside the lake some distance away, fishing. They waved at him. He smiled to hear them chattering, the water reflecting and carrying the sound. He could make out enough of their words to know that Dena was telling the young woman all about his adventures.

He pulled on his gunbelt. Even though he had seen no evidence of anyone around, it was just the time when somebody was bound to turn up. He went to check the rabbit snares he'd left earlier and brought six hares to the lakeside. He fumbled at his ankle, then remembered his knife had been confiscated by Sheriff Sikes. With a curse he fetched another from his saddlebag and skinned and cleaned the rabbits. After peeling some green branches for roasting, he carried pine boughs over to the hollow log and lit them, then blew a cloud of fragrant heavy smoke into the hive. The angry buzzing became a low hum. The bees, drugged with smoke, crawled peaceably over his arm as he reached inside and broke off large pieces of the fresh white comb. He caught two stings on his neck as he was retreating, but figured it was worth it.

Dena and Julie returned to the campsite with two trout, and they set to preparing supper. As she bustled around the camp, Julie MacKenzie seemed transformed from the sullen, sad-eyed girl he'd first spotted in the hotel lobby, to a willowy, high-spirited woman. She'd changed from the yellow gingham dress to a leather riding skirt of Dena's and a pair of Dena's boots that seemed to fit all right, as well as a red flannel shirt of Fargo's. The color of the shirt set off the creamy paleness of her neck and the blush of her cheeks. Fargo found himself watching her with pleasure as her slim form bent down to arrange the thick logs. Her narrow waist set off the plump fullness of her high breasts and the roundness of her hips. She was not unaware of his attention and caught him staring at her several times, returning his interest with a smile.

Just before the sunset Dena was off walking when Julie decided to have a quick bath in an inlet of the lake, not far on the other side of the rocks.

"Call if you need me," Fargo said with a smile.

"I expect I can manage," Julie said with a giggle.

Fargo sat by the fire as the sun touched on the mountains and the shadows grew long across the lake. A few high clouds turned apricot, then molten gold, then ruddy, as the sun slipped away. Suddenly, he became aware that something was wrong. What? He listened, but heard nothing unusual—the call of a lark out late, the lap of water on the shore. He heard Julie splashing in the inlet just out of sight. He rose slowly, his hand on his Colt, suddenly worried about her. Yes, it was about Julie. He felt the presence of someone. He looked all around the lake as far as he could see, his eyes searching the dark lip of the forest. If there was someone watching, he could not be seen. Fargo moved from the campsite back into the edge of the forest, walking as quietly as wind. Then, his eyes and ears alert, he moved slowly over the slight rise past the rocks until he could see the inlet.

There Julie stood, knee deep in the lake, naked as Eve. Her pale body with its extravagant curves was outlined against the lake, which reflected the last pink of sunset. His eyes drank in the sight of her rose-tipped breasts, her delicately rounded belly, and the pale golden triangle of fur between her soft rounded thighs. Reluctantly, he tore his eyes away, looking past her at the far lake shore, his blue eyes searching the dark pines of the slope above the lake all the way to the rocky ridge at the top. Did something move there, or did he only imagine it? Fargo stood watching as the light faded from rose to blue.

"Why, Skye Fargo!" Julie's voice roused him. She had spotted him standing among the trees, waded ashore, and now held his shirt clutched in front of her. He stepped out and went to meet her.

"I thought . . ." he started, then decided he didn't want to frighten her. "Wondered if you needed somebody to wash your back," he said with a grin.

"Spying on me like that," Julie complained, but she sounded more flattered than angry. "I expected better of you. You're as bad as my brothers. Now get."

Julie turned her back on him and treated him to a full view of her rear end, high and rounded. She fluffed her hair with one hand and glanced back at him over one shoulder.

"Can I get dressed now?"

"I'm not stopping you." He laughed, running his eyes over her again. He retreated to beyond the rocks so that she was out of sight but not far away. Meanwhile, the uneasy feeling hadn't left him. There was nothing to tell him that anything was out of place. No sound. No smell. But something had moved high up on the hillside. Deer, maybe?

Bear? After long years in the wilderness, a man learned to trust his instincts.

Julie came around the rock, all dressed, her damp hair clinging to her neck. She stopped short to see him standing there, then came up and stood very close to him, as if daring him to touch her. Fargo reached out and pulled her toward him, her slender waist so familiar by now. She clung to him, her breasts pillow soft against his hard chest.

He held her chin in his hand, then kissed her, parting her sweet lips insistently with his tongue. She sucked his tongue into her mouth, hungrily, stroking it with her own, open, wanting, willing. She was more experienced than he'd expected. He slipped his hand inside her shirt and massaged the hard nipple. She moaned, and he felt the hardness in his Levi's throbbing with desire. He wanted to be inside her, moving back and forth inside the pink folds of that pale golden triangle. His hands moved downward and cupped her round buttocks, pulling her harder against him so she could feel the hard rod of his swollen desire against the mound of her womanliness. His hips pushed against her rhythmically as his tongue continued to explore her mouth. He pulled away, and she gasped, breathing hard.

"I wanted you to watch me in the lake," Julie said. "Yes, please. I want you inside me, Skye."

3

There were times in a man's life when he just had to say to hell with the danger, and this was one of them. Fargo felt the throbbing between his legs as he held the soft curves of Julie MacKenzie in his arms.

"Yes, now," she murmured, her fingers in his hair, tickling his ears.

Fargo pulled her toward a cleft in the rocks where they would be hidden from view, backed her up against a rock, and bent to kiss her again. Her mouth, sweet and willing, pulled his tongue inside. She moved her hips against his insistently, beneath their clothing, and he felt her mound against the hard rod of his desire. Desperately, her hands fumbled at his belt as he pulled her skirt up around her waist and slipped his hands inside her bloomers, pulling them down. She stepped out of them. He cupped the warm roundness of her buttocks as, button by button, she undid his Levi's, then pulled them down his hips.

"Oh, yes," she muttered as her fingers found and stroked his huge hardness, back and forth. Fargo throbbed with a kind of sweet pain to be inside her. Suddenly, he lifted her up onto a shelf of the rock. She cried out in surprise as he pulled up her skirt further. Then she smiled and spread her legs wide. She lay back, open before him, the moist pink folds among the golden fur of her triangle. She smiled up at him, tugging at the buttons of her shirt to expose her large, pink-tipped breasts. He covered them with his hands, feeling the softness of her, gently massaging the nipples, as the head of his huge cock pushed at the very entrance of her, waiting in sweet agony.

"Oh, God," Julie breathed. "Yes, Skye, yes."

He began to push inside her, slow inch by slow inch, as she widened to take in the length of him. He ground his hips into her as Julie clenched her fists. She was hot, wet, tight around him, taking in his full length, deeper and deeper into her. He grabbed her hips and began stroking in and out as she lay before him on the shelf of rock, and he stood between her lovely white legs. Harder and harder he plunged, holding her hips against him. She moved her hands to her own breasts, her eyes on his. He moved one hand to the sweet button above her entrance and tickled her there, teasing at first, then more insistently.

"Ah—ah," she gasped, her back arching upward and her thighs opening more to him, her juices flowing in her slick tunnel as he plunged in and out. The explosion gathered in him, the insistent urgency. She bucked, and he felt her suddenly go tense all over. Her eyes closed, and he felt her contractions as she came, as if she were sucking him in, sucking him dry. His spasms of ecstasy began, shooting up inside her, over and over again. The waves of release kept coming, squirting his hotness into her, pumping into her wetness, until there was nothing left. He slowed, reluctant to leave her.

"Oh, oh, Skye," she moaned, shivering.

He lifted her toward him, and she wrapped her arms around his neck and her legs around his waist as he held her, feeling their hot connectedness. Her heart pounded against his chest for long minutes as she clung to him. Then he let her down gently onto the rock shelf and pulled up his Levi's. Julie seemed unable to move, but lay back on the rock. She blinked at him and smiled.

"That was better than I could ever have imagined," she said, sitting up reluctantly and buttoning her shirt. Fargo heard a crackle of footsteps on gravel from the direction of the campfire and knew Dena had returned. As he and Julie emerged from the rock crevice, he scanned the dark forests on the slopes above the lake. The feeling of danger had gone away, but somehow he knew it had not been his imagination.

They returned to the campfire hand in hand. Dena, spearing rabbits on the skewers and propping them over the flames, grinned when she saw them, then grew sober. Her rifle lay beside her, and her pistol was jammed into her belt.

Dena raked her fingers through her silver hair and donned her hat. She gave Fargo a sharp look, and then her eyes went beyond him to the surrounding hills. He nodded, a complete understanding between them. Dena was as suspicious as he was. The Shoshoni part of her had an instinct for the wilds. And she felt something out there too.

"I'm going to have another look around," Dena said curtly. "Save me some."

Before he could protest, she'd gone off, rifle in hand. The light was fading from the sky, and the night turned cold. The cloud bank in the west moved slowly across the few stars. Fargo built up the fire and settled in with his back resting against the warmed rock and one arm around Julie. She rotated the sizzling rabbit over the flames and occasionally lifted them off the fire.

Julie nestled in close and fed him another piece of meat, holding it teasingly in front of him until he snapped it from her fingers. She giggled.

But Fargo's thoughts were far away. Dena had been gone a half hour. The clouds had blown in quickly, covering the night sky, and the wind was high. Fargo had begun to wish he'd talked her out of going off alone. But then he told himself Dena could damn well take care of herself. She'd been traveling the West solo for years. Nobody could get the better of Deadeye Dena. The idea that somebody was out there bothered him again. He listened to the sound of a hoot owl, which ceased abruptly. Julie noticed his preoccupation.

"What is it?" she asked. "You hear something?"

"I'll have some more," he said to distract her. But she wasn't fooled.

"You mean that owl?" she said. "Maybe it was some kind of signal. Indians, maybe?"

Fargo shook his head. No, the owl was real. It

was just the interrupted call, as if it had been startled. He wondered where Dena was and then tried to imagine who was out there in the trees. If somebody was watching them, he'd have figured there were three of them, and he'd wonder where Dena had got to. That would put him on his guard, making it all the harder for Dena to sneak up on him. The thought must have occurred to Dena too because Fargo heard her footsteps coming around the shore. She was making no attempt to walk quietly.

"I hear somebody coming," Julie whispered, her eyes wide with fright.

"Nothing to worry about," Fargo said. "It's Dena. She and I are just being extra careful." Julie relaxed as Dena's familiar wiry form strode into the firelight.

"Nice walk?" Fargo asked, his voice louder than usual.

They exchanged looks, and she shook her head subtly. No, she'd seen nothing, heard nothing definite. But he could tell from the tenseness in her body that she was still keyed up.

Dena sat down. With her gnarled fingers she pulled some honey-broiled rabbit from a skewer. Her eyes were thoughtful as she stared into the fire. Her face, scored as deep as desert cliffs, told a story of hard living and hard riding. Dena was a woman determined to show the world she could survive in the wild on her wits and her trigger finger. And she had. But tonight there was a kind of wistful remembering in her eyes that Fargo'd never seen before. Julie noticed it too.

"Is there something wrong, Dena?" she asked shyly.

"This was Shoshoni land once," Dena said at last. Julie looked puzzled, and Dena caught her expression. "I'm part Shoshoni, was raised Shoshoni until I was twenty. Then my white relatives got ahold of me again and took me down to Cheyenne to civilize me. Guess that didn't work!" She laughed her usual harsh bark and pulled off more meat. "After a few years of corsets and teacups, I ran away. Only I didn't fit in with my tribe anymore either. I've been wandering ever since."

"What was it like, being an Indian?" Julie asked.

"Being Shoshoni, you mean?" Dena's eyes looked faraway. "In those days we had this land all to ourselves. That was back when there weren't so many wagons coming west. The few that did made their way through the mountains just west of here, what we call the Old Gap now. That was before the Oregon Trail got established farther south. So the only white folks were trappers and traders. They knew enough to live like Shoshoni. They didn't change the land—they let the land change them. The only white I knew was a young fellow, a trapper named Pete Walker."

"Yellow Pete!" Julie said, clapping her hands delightedly. "I know him. He's a nice old man, kind of a hermit. He's a friend of my pa's. At least . . . he was when Pa was alive. He always came for Christmas."

"Why do you call him Yellow Pete?" Dena asked.

"One Christmas Ma had a whole bunch of carrots in the cellar, but the cellar froze and thawed,

66

and they were starting to go bad. She was pickling fast as she could. Pete decided he'd help out by eating 'em by the handful. And then he turned yellow as a sunflower in July."

It was Dena's turn to laugh. "That sounds like Pete Walker. I can't believe he's still alive."

The rest of the evening they stayed by the fire, talking. Whoever was out there, Fargo decided, probably wouldn't rush them, but would wait until they'd gone to sleep. As they prepared to bed down for the night, Fargo took Dena aside and told her he'd take the watch. Dena got out her blankets and put them close by the fire, making two beds. She motioned to Julie to help. Julie looked longingly toward Fargo. He spread his bedroll at the edge of the circle of firelight where there were several rocks the size of a man's head lying around. Nearby was a gap between two of the encircling rocks. Tired, even after a day's rest, they turned in early. Fargo kicked some dirt over the fire to kill the flames. He needed darkness.

After they lay still for half an hour, Fargo could tell by Julie's steady breathing that she'd fallen asleep. And he also knew by the sound that Dena was not. The fire had died to embers. Slowly, he eased out of his bedroll. He pulled it over several of the rocks so it looked as if he was still inside. He put his hat on one of the rocks and left it to look like his head, then silently slipped out between the gap. Dena murmured to him to let him know she knew he was up and about.

For the next two hours Fargo moved as slowly as a shadow from rock to rock and tree trunk to tree trunk. He was pleased at how hidden their campsite was. The towering rocks hid them from all sides, and only a faint, reflected red glow showed where the fire was. To spot them, you had to be practically right on top of the site. He stood for a long time in the darkness, completely still, watching and listening to the night.

The wind made the fir trees murmur and creak. He heard the hoot of the great horned owl, then the two notes of the burrowing owl. A couple of does and a buck came down to the water to drink, then wandered back into the woods. Bats fluttered occasionally overhead. A gray cloud cover hid the moon, so there was hardly any light. Then Fargo spotted him.

In the deep shadow of the trees halfway around the lake, there was a movement. Fargo stared at it until the spots swam before his eyes, then blinked and looked again. He wasn't mistaken. The man moved again. It was one man, alone, moving in complete silence just inside the edge of the forest. He was making for the campsite. Fargo calculated the stranger would pass just in front of him before crossing the open space toward the ring of rocks. During the next hour the man made his careful, silent, and almost invisible approach. And Fargo stayed absolutely still, not daring to even draw his gun.

This stranger knew the ways of the night. He waited until a gust of wind stirred the trees before moving forward in small, darting motions. And he had infinite patience, never hurrying, making his slow way, watchful, wary, all senses alert. Fargo, hidden behind a tree trunk, waited and watched as the man came nearer.

He was small. That was all Fargo could make out, except for the shape of the barrel of his rifle. The man ducked behind a tree and waited for five minutes. Then he moved again, ten feet away from where Fargo stood. The man paused, watching, turning his head from side to side as he listened to the night. He was good all right. He was damned good. Then, as the wind roared up again and the trees whispered and creaked, the stranger darted forward, a dark shadow in the shadow of the woods. He stopped behind a tree just in front of Fargo and peered out toward the campsite.

In a whisper of movement Fargo's Colt was in his hand at the same instant he spoke.

"Drop it or so help me, I'll blow your brains out."

Fargo felt the stranger turn to stone in front of him.

"Drop it," Fargo said again.

The man did, and Fargo moved forward, pushing him against a tree, jamming the barrel of his Colt into the man's back.

"Walk forward," Fargo commanded. "Into camp. Slow and steady. Trip and I'll shoot you." He'd retrieve the man's rifle later. If he bent down just now, the wily stranger would use that moment to his advantage.

The small man did as he was told. As they approached the camp, Fargo kicked a few stones to alert Dena. When they rounded the rocks and came into sight of the fire, she was crouched behind a boulder, a pistol in each hand. Dena rose when she saw them. Julie tossed in her sleep beside the fire.

As the ruddy light from the embers hit them, Fargo was surprised to see a grizzled old man, his face deep etched, but his eyes bright and his body taut as a bowstring. He wore a strange conglomeration of clothing—buckskins with a tatter of plaid flannel underneath, a patchwork of denim on his elbows and knees. His unkempt gray hair gave him a wild appearance.

"Who the hell are you?" Dena shot at him, her voice edged with exasperation.

"You first," he shot back.

Julie woke up to the sound of their voices and sat up in surprise.

"Yellow Pete!" she said. "What are you doing here?"

She jumped up and ran to him, giving him a hug. He looked embarrassed by her attentions.

"Came to rescue you," he said, abashed. "But I got myself caught at it."

"Rescue me?" Julie said. "But these are friends, Pete." Fargo lowered his Colt, as did Dena. "This is Deadeye Dena, Fastest Lady Shootist in the West," Julie said with a touch of pride. Dena stepped forward to shake his hand.

"We met already, Pete," she said. "Long time back. You knew me as Summer Cloud." Pete took a startled step backward.

"Summer Cloud?" He rubbed his eyes in disbelief. "That was a hundred years ago, when the Shoshoni and me had this land all to ourselves."

70

"Damned right," Dena said. Pete looked her over again.

"Well, you used to be a pretty thing. Hell, you've got old, girl," he said at last.

"And you used to be a handsome buck. Now you look worn-out as a used saddle," she snapped. Pete laughed and scratched his grizzled head.

"Guess I do at that, now."

"And who might you be, young fellow?" Pete glowered at Fargo. "You're damned good at sneaking up on a man. When I spotted you this morning coming into my valley, I paid no attention till I recognized Miss Julie here. I figured you must a' kidnapped her. Then I caught sight of you peeping at her while she was bathing in the lake—"

"What?" Julie exclaimed, blushing. "*You* were watching me too? Good God, seems like the whole territory's saw me buck naked."

"I won't ask what you were doing watching," Fargo said to the old man. "I'm Skye Fargo." At his name, Yellow Pete's jaw dropped.

"Skye Fargo," he repeated wonderingly. "Hell, ain't *that* a coincidence? MacKenzie and I had a business deal, and you're part of it. He was going down to Hell's Picket to fetch you up here on July first. Where is old MacKenzie, anyway?"

"Pa's dead," Julie said. "Fell out of the hayloft and broke his neck."

"The hell you say." Pete swore a string of colorful curses and scratched his scalp again. His gray hair stood on end. "MacKenzie wasn't the kind to die that stupid. Must have to do with that bad lot that's been visiting your ranch the last month or so. I seen 'em hanging around, and they're just the kind of folks I don't like. MacKenzie and I usually rendezvoused at a stream we knew about once a week. But he ain't come the last month or so. I just figured he was busy."

Julie told Pete all about Sam Blade and the note on the ranch and on the cattle. And all about Blade's gang of men terrorizing the family. With every word Pete's face grew blacker, and he sat, twisting the end of his beard between his fingers. When they'd finished talking, it was late in the night.

"So, all we gotta do is sit tight and let that posse catch up with us," Pete said. "Then Miss Julie here can tell 'em what's been goin' on."

"I've been thinking about that," Fargo said. "The problem is, Sam Blade swore he'd kill the rest of the MacKenzies if Julie told the truth. I don't know if he's with the posse or not, but if he somehow got wind of it—"

"Oh, no!" Julie said.

"That's right," Fargo said. "There's no telling what Blade would do if he got desperate. That's a chance we can't take. Our only hope is to beat 'em back to the ranch before Blade figures out what we're doing. We'll get the family loose, and then let the posse catch up. Then we can get this whole thing straightened out once and for all. Meanwhile, let's get some sleep," Fargo said. "Tomorrow, we're moving on."

"If you folks don't mind," Pete said, "I'll fetch my rifle and take my boots off here tonight."

Dena threw him a blanket, and they settled in.

The fire was almost out. Julie and then Dena dropped off to sleep, but Fargo's thoughts kept him awake. Fargo turned over to spot Yellow Pete sitting on his blanket, staring out across the lake, twisting his beard. Something big was bothering the old man.

Fargo rose silently as the first birds began to twitter. Morning mist rose on the lake, and the distant peaks flushed pink with the first rays of dawn. His feet led him up between the trees, where night still lingered beneath them. He continued climbing the pine slope until he came out on the rocky ridge overlooking the lake.

From here he had a good view of the surrounding mountains and thick forests. He looked back toward the east and the series of hills they had come through and saw a smudge of smoke on the horizon, a faint yellowing across the sky. Fargo swore softly to himself as he calculated the distance—no more than fifteen miles. And a pretty big campfire. It could be anybody—wandering trappers, a band of Shoshoni on the move, some homesteaders. But Fargo felt certain it was the Hell's Picket posse. Somehow, Sikes and his men had picked up the trail. They had to get a move on. And now.

Just as Fargo was about to descend, a movement at the far end of the lake caught his eye. In a flash he saw the figure of a man in buckskins, standing almost invisibly beside a tree. For a moment he thought it might be Yellow Pete, but even at that distance, he knew somehow it wasn't. The man was looking in the direction of the campsite.

Suddenly, as if he felt himself being watched, the man stepped behind a tree and disappeared.

Fargo swore again. He suspected he had just spotted the reason the posse had found their trail. They had an Indian scout—and a damned good one—somebody sent ahead of the posse to track them, somebody who really knew the ways of the woods. If he could get his hands on the scout, the posse would be virtually blind. He started down the slope, running hard, angling through the trees as he worked his way around the lake toward the spot where he had seen the scout. As he drew nearer, he slowed, moving cautiously from tree to tree, ears and eyes alert.

A half hour later, he had combed the woods near the place he had last spotted the man, but had seen nothing. He found the soft indentation of moccasins. Warily, he followed the tracks into the forest until he came to a small clearing where a horse had been tethered. Fargo stood reading the tracks. The horse had been shod, so maybe the man wasn't Indian. Or maybe he was just riding a white man's horse. What was perfectly clear was that the scout had taken off in a big hurry. The horse's tracks led off at a fast gallop through the trees. And that in itself was a bad sign—a very bad sign. Fargo hurried back to the campsite and met three relieved faces.

"We were just organizing a search party," Dena said. Fargo hastily told them what he had seen, and within minutes they had packed up the camp.

"Up that ridge there's a way out of this valley," Pete said. "It's a damn sight better 'n running into that posse on your way out of here. I'll show you the way. We'll pass right by my place, and I'll fetch us two more horses. Julie and I will need 'em."

"You coming with us?" Dena asked. She sounded pleased.

"Durn right I am," Pete said. "Fargo's going to clean out those hornets that's came to nest at the MacKenzie ranch. Well, that's a fight I'd like to be a part of. And, anyway, me and Fargo have some business to take care of too."

Fargo looked quizzically at Pete, wondering what kind of business he was talking about, but the old man ignored him and turned away. Well, Pete would talk in his own good time. When the saddlebags were packed, Fargo and Julie mounted the Ovaro, and Pete got up awkwardly behind Dena on her palomino. She started forward and he almost fell off.

"Hold on, you old man," Dena snapped. Pete shyly put his hands around her waist. With Pete giving directions, the horses climbed back and forth, up through the trees, until they reached the rocky ridge where Fargo had been earlier. They paused, and Fargo noted that the smoke smudge he had seen earlier was gone now. The fire must have been put out. That meant the posse was on the move.

"Look there," Fargo said. Far below, crossing a high mountain meadow, was a long train of men and horses. They were coming fast.

"Whew," Pete said. "Looks like they got half the town coming after you. I guess they take hangings pretty seriously in Hell's Picket."

They turned away and continued along the ridge until they came to a solid rock face that seemed to open outward as they approached until an opening became visible, wide enough for one rider at a time to pass through. They rode single file between the overhanging rock and emerged in a small valley, lush with fir and a flowering meadow. Near a babbling brook a small cabin and stable stood beneath some sheltering trees. Pete hurried into his paddock and led out a docile gray for Julie. He mounted a spirited Appaloosa with saddlebags and a scabbard for his rifle.

"I hate to do this, but I guess this is as good a time as any to shut my back door," Pete said. He pulled his rifle up and turned back toward the narrow rock passageway where they had entered the valley. He aimed up high, and Fargo saw what he was after and pulled his own rifle up. Dena gave a whoop and did the same, all three of them aiming at a small mound of rocks that held a huge boulder precariously balanced high on the slopes above the narrow opening.

The rocks splintered and flew about. The gigantic boulder teetered, then rocked, tipped, and rolled forward, crashing down the slope, bouncing against other rocks as the landslide grew. The mountainside gave way, and the air filled with the roar of tumbling stones.

"Come on!" Pete shouted over the tumult. They galloped across the meadow to the far edge, then paused to look back. Through the rising dust they could see a huge pile of stones where the entrance to the valley had been. "They'll know where we went, but there'll be no way to get their horses over that." Pete laughed. "They'll have to go all the way back around the mountain, and that will give us a good day's lead."

Fargo led as they followed the stream downhill, descending quickly through the thick forest. All day long they rode the horses hard. Fargo stayed well out in front of them, looking for anyone ahead on the trail. But the land seemed deserted. Just after nightfall they reached a post driven into the ground with an *M* branded into it.

"This is the boundary of our ranch," Julie said proudly.

"Let's get off the trail," Fargo said. They plunged into the forest and rode another half hour through the woods and along the edges of mountain meadows. It was good land. Finally, as the moon rose, they came to the edge of a grove and saw below a wide, rich valley. In the distance Fargo saw the dark herd of cattle and heard the low murmur of occasional lowing. They dismounted and tethered the horses and lay down at the top of a hill to look down on the ranch.

Below was a road leading to the entrance of the compound. There were paddocks and stables, as well as a large barn. A two-story ranch house stood in the center, the windows golden with light. In the shadows of the front porch, Fargo spotted two men standing watch. Suddenly, one of the dark figures crossed the yard and stood by the barred gate for a long time, listening and watching. Then he returned to his post on the front porch, and the other made a circle around the house. Damn, they were being careful, Fargo thought.

There was a small flare of light as the other man lit a cigarette. Then the front door opened, spilling a yellow path of light across the yard. Two men came out, and the other two went inside. Fargo watched as one walked slowly around the house, and then the other stood by the front gate, watching and listening. After watching for a few minutes, he understood the pattern of their watch.

Fargo considered their options. Julie had said Blade had ten men. There was no way to overpower them. The most important thing now was to get the MacKenzie family to safety. And then they'd wait until Sheriff Sikes and his posse showed up. If he could just get the family spirited away. Around the back of the ranch was a wooden slope, where one finger of dark trees reached toward the compound. Using the trees as cover, he could get within a few hundred yards of the ranch house. A plan formed in his mind. He motioned them all back into the shelter of the woods, where he found out from Julie what he needed to know.

"You got any whiskey, Dena?" he asked.

"I hardly think this is time for a toast, Fargo," she snapped.

"Get it," he said. Dena fetched a flask from her saddlebag and handed it to him. He removed the top, sniffed it, then poured some of it out over Yellow Pete's shirt.

"Hey," Pete said. "I guess you got something in mind, Fargo."

"Yeah," Fargo said. "This whiskey will do just fine."

An hour later, Fargo was inching forward in the yellow grass, having left the cover of the trees. He paused, his eyes on the dark shape of the ranch house. The downstairs windows were illuminated, and the sounds of men's voices came out. It sounded like a poker game. As he watched, the last of the upstairs windows went dark. Julie's mother, Pauline MacKenzie, had gone to bed. And the boy, Jimmy, and the little girl, Hanna, were asleep too. It was time to make his move.

Fargo waited until he saw the dark figure of the guard making his circuit around the house. Then he eased to his feet and, hunched low, sprinted silently toward the house. He spotted the ladder just where Julie said it would be, leaning in a dark corner back by the stone chimney. That would come in handy later. He listened to the rough voices from inside. He counted eight men playing poker. Suddenly, he heard the low voices of the guards at the front of the house, and he pressed himself into the shadowy wall. A moment later, he heard the crunch of gravel under boots as one of the men headed across the yard to stand by the front gate for a while.

Silently, Fargo leapt up onto the porch railing and hoisted himself up onto the roof, his powerful arms raising him slowly upward. As he rolled onto the roof, he dislodged a wooden shingle. Before he could make a grab for it, it noisily slipped down the pitched roof and clattered to the ground. Fargo froze.

"What the hell was that?" he heard a voice call out. There came the sound of approaching footsteps, moving warily, and the whisper of a pistol leaving its holster. Fargo didn't move as the man walked below, back and forth, just out of sight below the roofline. Fargo thought fast, then made the sound of a barn owl, a soft ascending wheezy cry. He waited a moment, then repeated it.

It worked. He heard the man walking away toward the front of the house.

"It's all right. It's goddamn owls," the man called out to the other guard.

Fargo waited another minute, then crawled slowly up the porch roof toward the window. He eased the window open and stepped in over the sill. The moonlight spilled across the floor, and his eyes made out the shape of a double bed. He heard the sound of soft breathing. In another instant he stood over it, looking down on Pauline MacKenzie. Even in the dim light he could tell she was as beautiful as her daughter, Julie, but entirely different. Pauline's long straight hair lay in silken waves on her pillow, dark and lush, and her brows were dramatically arched. Her nightgown gaped open, and he could see the curve of one breast as she nestled under the patchwork quilt. Fargo leaned over and put his hand firmly over her mouth.

Pauline MacKenzie was awake in an instant, flailing, kicking, and trying to scream. She lashed out, and a china pitcher standing next to the bed on a washstand teetered, then fell to the floor in a crash. Down below, there was a sudden silence, then the sound of chairs being pushed back and heavy footsteps. There wasn't a moment to lose. Fargo lay down on top of her and spoke in her ear.

"Calm down. I'm a friend. I've come to help you get away."

Her reaction was immediate. She stopped struggling and nodded her head. Fargo removed his hand and looked for a place to hide. The bed was too low to the ground. He heard the pounding of feet in the hallway. With only a second to spare, he dove under the quilt. Pauline half sat up, and he could feel her arranging the quilt and the pillows over him as the door burst open.

"What the hell was that?" a gruff voice demanded.

Beneath the covers Fargo lay tangled in Pauline's nightdress, his face pressed against the musky sweetness of her thigh. He was sunk deep into the thick feather mattress, but even so, Slade's men might think the shape under the quilt looked a little odd.

"It's all right, Billy," she snapped. "I just had a bad dream. And I knocked over the pitcher here. Now, get out of my room." That was fast thinking, Fargo said to himself. He inhaled the sweet perfume of her and felt himself harden. He didn't dare move.

The men retreated, and the door closed. Fargo started to come up for air when Pauline spoke again.

"I said get out. That means you, Billy Guire."

Fargo heard the man approach the bed.

"Now, come on, Miz MacKenzie," the gruff

voice said. "You know what you're going to get soon as Sam Blade gets back here. You and that fire-headed daughter of yours too. Why, we're going to have ourselves one helluva party with you two ladies. Every last one of us. Why, we've been without any ass for a whole month. That's going to feel real good, now that your old man's gone." Fargo felt Pauline shudder. "Now, don't you want me just to warm you up a little?"

Fargo was just about to leap out from under the covers when he felt Pauline lash out at Billy. He heard a resounding slap.

"Try that again, and I'll tell Blade," she spat. "You know he's got first dibs on me. He'd kill you if you touched me first."

"You bitch," Billy said. "You bitch. You'll pay for this." His footsteps retreated across the room, and Fargo heard the door slam shut. Pauline seemed paralzyed, and Fargo lay long minutes until the sound of the poker game resumed. Then he threw the quilt aside and pulled her to her feet.

"Who are you?" she whispered. She clung to him for a moment, and he felt her trembling like a leaf, and he knew she was about to cry.

"There's no time for that now," he said. "Trust me. I'm going to get you and your kids to safety. Just do as I say."

Pauline took a deep breath, and Fargo knew she would be all right. In five minutes she had awakened the boy, Jimmy, a towheaded kid of about thirteen who didn't look a bit scared, but eyed Fargo curiously. She held the little girl, Hanna, in her arms as they stood at the window in their nightshirts and shoes. There was no time to dress, and Pauline held their clothes bundled in her hand. Each of the beds had been left with piled blankets beneath the quilts so it looked like they were still sleeping there.

Fargo glanced up at the moon. Yes, it was just about time. Everything was going according to plan. He whispered his instructions, and then got them all out onto the roof, where they huddled against the wall, waiting. Hanna held her mother's hand, her eyes big as saucers. They didn't have long to wait. In ten minutes there came the sound of hoofbeats on the road and a loud, drunken voice.

"Oh, my darlin' Clementine," Yellow Pete sang at the top of his lungs.

The guards ran toward the gate. The poker game came to a screeching halt, and the front door to the ranch house was flung open. Fargo moved like lightning under the cover of the hub-bub. He leapt down from the roof and grabbed the ladder. In a moment the boy scrambled down. Hanna followed, her little feet searching for the rungs. Meanwhile, the ruckus in the front yard continued.

"Well, if I ain't in Hell's Picket, where the hell am I?" Pete shouted. "I musta taken a wrong turn somewhere. Where the hell is town? You sure this ain't Hell's Picket?"

"He smells like a still," one of the men muttered.

"Let's just knock him off," another said.

"He's harmless." It was Billy Guire. "Get him back on his horse and outta here."

"Let's have a little fun," one of the men shouted. A sudden pistol shot resounded in the night. Fargo, holding the ladder, swore to himself. Hell, he knew it was dangerous to send Pete in. But it was the only chance they had. What were they doing to the old man?

At the sound of the gunfire, Hanna froze on the ladder. Fargo reached up and grabbed her around the waist and swung her down. Pauline followed quickly as another shot rang out and then a third.

"Make a run for the trees," Fargo told them. "Dena's waiting there to guide you to the horses up on the ridge. Stay low and keep moving."

Pauline grabbed her children's hands, and the three of them made a run for it. Fargo drew his Colt and edged around the side of the ranch house toward the raucous crowd, cursing Sam Blade's gang of roughs. There was the sound of cruel laughter and more gunfire, a horse rearing, and Pete shouting. If they'd hurt the old man, Fargo swore to himself, he'd take on the lot of them. All of 'em. Right now. No matter what the consequences.

4

Colt in hand, Fargo slid around the corner of the ranch house as sadistic laughter, gunfire, and the stamp of the horse's feet sounded through the still night air. Yellow Pete shouted out. Fargo swore silently as he paused at the edge of the building and peered around into the wide yard.

There he saw the crowd of Sam Blade's men gathered around Pete on his horse. Two men were holding the bridle, and others were shooting close to the horse's head. The Appaloosa was bucking in fear and pain. Pete was holding on for dear life, but he looked okay.

"Give him a good scare, then let 'im go," Billy Guire shouted. "His horse'll be stone deaf and so scared he'll run all the way to Kansas before he stops. That'll teach the son of a bitch." Fargo felt the rage well up within him at the sight of the men torturing the horse with the loud gunfire. His finger tightened on the trigger as he calculated his odds. Yeah, he could take out six of 'em before he'd have to reload. But one of them would get Pete. And then the chances of the MacKenzie family getting away were next to nothing. Suddenly, with a loud cheer, the men let go of the bridle. Pete's horse took off in a wild gallop out the gate and down the road. Pete shouted incoherently, still pretending to be drunk. Slade's men laughed and shot their guns off as Pete disappeared down the road.

"He'll think twice before taking a wrong turn again," Billy said and laughed.

Fargo breathed a sigh of relief, retraced his steps, and replaced the ladder in the corner by the chimney. He had just finished when he heard footsteps approaching. There was no time to hide. Fargo pressed himself into the deep shadow by the chimney as one of the men came into view. He was walking slowly, looking out into the trees. Fargo peered in the direction where Pauline and the children had disappeared. He didn't see any movement. They must have got to cover. The guard stopped and fumbled in his shirt pocket, then pulled out a cigarette and lit it. He stood for long minutes, smoking and looking out over the quiet landscape. Fargo hoped Dena had her eye on the guard and was keeping them all still. One movement, one noise, and the game would be up. Finally, the man finished, dropped the butt on the ground, and continued his round. Fargo waited a moment, and was just starting to move forward when the sound of an approaching horse stopped him. He melted back into the shadows, wondering who would ride up to the ranch this late. The guards ran toward the front, and the others moved out onto the porch. He heard the sound of jingle-bobs and knew it was Sam Blade.

"Welcome back, Blade!" one of them called out.

"Hey, where's the cute little redhead girl?"

Fargo felt a wave of surprise. What was Blade doing back here at the ranch so soon? He moved forward until he could see the yard and Blade dismounting. At the sight of his tall figure, Fargo felt the hatred rise in him. Blade strode across the yard and stood in front of the porch.

"Who the hell was that riding out of here?" Blade asked. "Some old man I passed on the road galloping like the devil was biting his tail?"

"Old drunk," Bill Guire answered. "He took a wrong turn, so we scared him off."

"You should have shot him," Blade retorted. "All right, men, there's been a change of plans."

"Did you get the map?" one of them called out.

"Got it right here," Blade retorted, patting his pocket. Fargo wondered if that was what MacKenzie had been going to retrieve from the bank safe in Hell's Picket. "But first," Blade continued, "we got ourselves a little problem. A problem by the name of Skye Fargo."

At the sound of his name, the men muttered among themselves, and Blade filled them in on what had happened in Hell's Picket.

"I sent Ponca out to scout for the posse," Blade said. Fargo thought of the buckskinned figure he'd spotted at the lake. That must have been Ponca. "So, Ponca sent word that Fargo's heading this way. Ponca's going to send the posse off in the wrong direction, and they'll be lost for a week. He'll rendezvous with us here in the morning. First thing, we're going to shoot the dame and the kids and get outta here. We'll hunt down Fargo and the girl, shoot her, and string him up. By the time Sheriff Sikes and his men catch up to us, we'll tell 'im how we found Fargo had killed the whole damn family. And we brought him to justice."

"Right," Bill Guire growled.

"But when are we going to get our money?" one of the men asked.

"Soon as that posse heads back to Hell's Picket," Blade said. He patted his pocket again. "Be patient, boys. We've got ourselves here a ticket to El Dorado." Sam Blade laughed and clapped Bill Guire on the back. The men went into the ranch house, leaving two of them on guard. Fargo slipped away into the night.

All the way back to the woods, Fargo's head was swimming with what he had heard. His plan to wait for the posse to help them wipe out Slade's gang had been foiled. The posse was being sent in the wrong direction by Slade's Indian scout, Ponca. And in the morning Slade and his men would discover that Pauline and the kids were missing. Then they'd swarm like angry bees. Fargo swore to himself as he reached the edge of the trees. He quickly climbed the hillside and found the others waiting by the horses. Pauline and the children had gotten dressed. She sat on a rock, cradling Hanna, who had fallen asleep. Jimmy stood protectively by his mother and Julie. Dena stood guard a little distance away, her rifle at the ready. Yellow Pete had returned too and was trying to calm his Appaloosa, who was skittish.

"Think she's gone deaf in one ear," Pete said. "The bastards." Fargo stroked the horse's neck and thought angrily of Blade's gang. They'd pay for this. They'd pay for the whole damn thing. When Fargo filled them in on what he'd overheard, Dena recognized Ponca's name.

"You know him?" Fargo asked.

"Yeah," she answered. "Ponca was a Shoshoni before the tribe exiled him. Lying, stealing, even murder—he's done it all. But one thing I'll say for Ponca. He was always a damn good tracker. He could track a snake across solid rock. If he's on our trail, we ain't got a snowball's hope in hell."

"Nobody tracks me," Yellow Pete said. "Why, we'll get him chasing his tail in no time."

"Yeah," Fargo said thoughtfully. "But the question is, where do we go? The posse's going to be wandering around in the wrong direction."

"If we head back to Hell's Picket," Dena pointed out, "the first man who spots Fargo will blow his head off. He's a wanted man."

"And Dena, you're wanted for helping me escape," Fargo added.

"I'm sorry we've caused all this trouble," Pauline said softly, her eyes full of tears. Fargo knew from the way Pauline looked at him that Julie had told her mother about him and about the murder of her son. "If only my husband hadn't been gambling and signed that note over to Sam Blade," Pauline said regretfully. "Mack never figured Blade would be interested in a ranch in the middle of nowhere. And when that agreement takes effect, Sam Blade's going to own the whole thing—the land, the cattle, everything. Blade's worked it out so that I have to make a big payment to the bank, no matter what, if I want my ranch back. Otherwise, Blade takes over, or the bank owns us."

"What is this about a map?" Fargo asked. Pauline shrugged her shoulders as Fargo told them what Sam Blade had said.

"Yeah, that map is partly what Mack wanted to talk to you about in Hell's Picket," Pete said. "It's about a gold shipment from Sutter's Mill."

"In California?" Fargo asked, disbelieving. "That's the mine that set off the gold rush of '49. But it's been played out for years."

"Well, when they first struck gold at Sutter's, nobody believed 'em," Pete recounted. "So they packed up a wagon full of a ton of gold, and they sent it east to Washington. Only it never arrived. It came through the Old Gap, and then just plumb disappeared!"

"And my tribe was blamed for it," Dena said bitterly.

"But what really happened," Pete continued, "was the men who were bringing it over got greedy. They had a quarrel, and then they ended up killing each other down to the last man."

"And this map shows where Sutter's lost gold is," Fargo said. "Too bad we can't get our hands on it." He glanced at Pauline. "That would solve all your problems."

"Oh, we don't need that map," Pete said. "Because I drew it. I found that gold, and I got the location all right up here." He tapped his forehead.

"I made the map for Mack in case anything ever happened to me."

"So, let's go get it," Jimmy piped up. It was the first time the boy had spoken. He was probably about twelve and sat next to his mother, listening and watching. She shushed him.

"Not so fast," Fargo said, smiling at the kid. "How come you didn't go after it before, Pete?"

"Mack and I had to wait until the first of July of this year," Pete said. "Eleven years to the day after Sutter's gold disappeared, the statute of limitations expired. And now it's finder's keeper's. It's only a day's ride from here out toward the Old Gap. That's why Mack called on you, Fargo. To help get that gold and get rid of Sam Blade."

"I don't want any gold," Pauline said firmly, patting Julie's hand. "I just want our ranch back. And I want my family safe."

Fargo sat in thought for a long minute, aware of the time ticking away, aware that down below at the ranch, Sam Blade's men were turning in for the night. Come morning, they would find Pauline and her kids had disappeared. And Ponca would ride in. Then the scout and Sam Blade's gang would be on their tails. He looked them all over—Pauline holding her little sleeping daughter, her dark eyes flashing defiance; Julie kneeling beside her, concern on her face; and the kid, Jimmy, watching Fargo with hope on his face. Dena and Pete stood beside the four horses. They were all depending on him. But how the hell could they get away now? It was a long way back to Hell's Picket, even if they could get there. And as soon as Blade and his men figured out that they were making for town, they'd head for the gold. And, hell, they'd get away with it, and the bank would end up owning the MacKenzie ranch. He swore silently. In another moment he'd made up his mind.

"All right," he said. "We're going start heading back to Hell's Picket. But Pete and I'll break away and head out toward the gold. Dena will take the rest of you into town, fast, no stopping. Sam Blade and his gang are bound to follow us, and you can make it to safety."

"But what about you?" Julie asked. "There are ten of them. And Sam Blade too."

"We'll be all right," Fargo assured her. In a couple of minutes he had them all on their horses. Julie with her younger sister on the gray, Dena with the boy on her palomino, and Pete alone on his Appaloosa—the horse was still nervous and balking. Fargo's Ovaro, strongest of all the horses, would carry him and Pauline for the time being. She wrapped her arms around his waist, and Fargo led off through the woods at a canter. The moon was already dropping down over the mountains. They had only a few hours more of darkness before the dawn came. And with it, more trouble.

Through the hours of traveling, Fargo kept his eyes open on the road ahead. He well remembered that the Indian scout, Ponca, would be heading toward the ranch toward dawn. If they had time, he'd stop and ambush the scout. But what if it failed and they lost the precious hours between themselves and Sam Blade's gang? He decided not to take the risk. They reached a long sage valley that lay between two ridges, as the sky began lightening in the east. Fargo hadn't seen a sign of the scout. They paused to let the horses have a drink.

"The turnoff to Sutter's gold is about ten miles ahead," Pete said, pointing to where the southern end of the valley was divided by a low hill that was surmounted by a field of scattered boulders.

"We'll stop there before we divide up," Fargo said. "You'll have to make a hard run straight to Hell's Picket," he added to Dena.

"We'll be fine," the old woman replied. "Just make sure that old strip of leather comes back to me in one piece." She nodded at Yellow Pete, who looked away, embarrassed but clearly pleased.

"Yeah, I'll do that," Fargo said with a laugh. The two old birds had obviously taken to each other. They were perfectly matched, one as tough and salty as the other.

They mounted and rode off again, the miles passing in a blur underneath the pounding hooves of the horses. On any other day Fargo would have enjoyed the purple distance of the nubby gray sage plain, the velvety folded hills, the tall blue peaks beyond, and the larks singing in the brush. As the sun rose, the light poured across the valley. They were galloping hard and were nearly to the fork in the trail when Fargo spotted the trouble. Pete saw it at the exact same moment and called out.

His keen eyes had caught a glitter of sun on the metal barrel of a rifle—way up among the boulders between the forks of the trail, waiting for them. He scanned the rocks and saw, here and there protruding from the rocks, the long dark shapes of rifle barrels. The men hiding up there had probably been watching their progress all the way down the long valley. Fargo swore. How did Sam Blade get his men out there ahead of them? Maybe Ponca had returned early, before dawn, found their tracks, and led the gang around a different route. There was nothing to be done now but ride like the devil. There was no chance to pull about and retreat. Dena galloped up beside him as the fork came up fast.

"Off to the left!" he shouted above the sound of the pounding hooves. Dena gave a wave and veered off, followed by Julie. The Ovaro's hooves bit the trail as he and Pete angled off to the right just as the pop of gunfire erupted from the rocks above. A couple of bullets whined by. Pauline's grip tightened on his waist, and Fargo suddenly realized he'd made a mistake. He'd meant to stop at the fork and send her off with her kids back to Hell's Picket and safety. Now, here she was going off with him and Pete toward the gold. And there was nothing to be done.

"I guess I'm coming with you now," she shouted to him.

The Ovaro's powerful legs pounded the earth. Fargo hunched down and felt Pauline do the same as they sped down the trail between the low bare hills. After an initial flurry the firing suddenly stopped. Fargo was puzzled. He glanced back and saw the hillside swarming with men. They seemed to be climbing the hill in a hurry, probably making their way back to their horses to give chase. He smiled to himself. It had worked. Sam Blade's men, seeing him and Pete heading toward the gold, had panicked. They wanted that lost gold shipment more than anything. And seeing somebody else going for it was putting them in a frenzy. Good, that was just what he wanted.

He glanced back to see Pete coming along on the Appaloosa. He was holding his shoulder, which was dark with blood. The old man had taken a bullet.

Fargo concentrated on the ride. The pinto was pulling hard, bearing up under the weight of the two of them. The yellow dusty trail wound between dun-colored hills, bare of scrub and littered here and there with outcroppings of black rock. Damn good spot for an ambush, Fargo thought. He considered turning and making a stand, but realized that with only him and Pete shooting, they didn't stand a chance.

"Can you shoot?" he shouted to Pauline.

"Sure can!" she said. "I was brought up on a ranch."

Even so, he thought, three against ten were terrible odds. Their best chance was to lead Sam Blade and his men on a wild-goose chase toward the gold so the others could get free. And, if they had a chance to snatch some of the booty to pay off the bank and save the ranch—well, he wouldn't count on that. In fact, he couldn't even count on being able to save their lives.

The trail opened out to a broad plain surrounded by low buff buttes and, in the distance, blue peaks dappled with white snow. The deep blue summer sky faded white as the sun rose higher. The dim trail disappeared in the yellow grass.

"Which way?" Fargo shouted back to Pete. The old man waved with one hand due west, then clutched his shoulder again.

"Ain't bleeding too bad," Pete shouted, seeing Fargo's concern. "Let's get some miles between us and them."

They set off across the wide yellow plain toward the dark forest and mountains far to the west. There was no place to hide, no way to disguise which way they'd gone, Fargo realized. They galloped hard, and Fargo looked back at the low hills they had come through. Sam Blade and his men had to be just behind them. He expected to see the dark throng of men emerge at any minute from the folded hills. But they never showed up.

The dark line of forest was right ahead when they came to a stream. Fargo reined in and dismounted, then helped Pauline down. She went to the stream to drink, as did the horses.

"Let's take a look at that shoulder," Fargo said to Pete. He tore away the shirt from the wound and saw the bullet had passed clean through the meat of the muscle. Fargo scooped up water in his hat and poured it over the blood-caked wound. Pete yelped, then bit his tongue and swore softly. Fargo pulled some clean moss from the riverbank to pack the wound.

"Let me help," Pauline said. She bent down and pulled up her riding skirt and tore a strip from the white cotton petticoat she wore underneath. In a moment they had Pete's shoulder wound dressed with moss. Pauline wound the cotton bandage and tied it expertly.

"I'll be fine now," Pete said, moving his shoulder back and forth gingerly. But Fargo read something else in his face. Pete nodded, and Fargo followed him, leaving Pauline by the horses. Pete's eyes swept the empty miles of barren yellow hills and the broad valley that lay behind them now. The silence and the solitude was eerie. There was no sign of pursuit. "I don't like it a bit," the old man said in a low voice so Pauline couldn't hear.

"Yeah," said Fargo. "I know what you mean. How the hell did Blade and his men set up that ambush back at the fork? They ought to be right behind us."

"Only thing I can think is they followed Dena, Julie, and the kids instead," Pete said, shaking his head. "Shit, I don't understand why."

"Don't say anything to her," Fargo said as his eyes lit on Pauline, who was rubbing down the horses. He silently blamed himself for the choice to keep to their plan of splitting up back at the ambush spot. He'd counted on the greed of Sam Blade's gang to get Sutter's lost gold to win out over any need for revenge on the MacKenzie family. But maybe he'd guessed wrong. And if he had, and Sam Blade's whole gang went chasing after Dena, Julie, and the kids . . . well, they were probably already dead. And now, even if he rode back after them, it would be too late. "Goddamn it," he said softly. Pete nodded, his face grim.

"Where to now?" Pete asked. Pauline overheard the question.

"Well, we're going straight off to pick up that gold, aren't we?" she said in a determined voice. She flicked her heavy dark hair over one shoulder. Even though she looked different from her red-headed daughter, Fargo saw that Pauline had the younger woman's defiance and spirit. Her black eyes glittered, her tawny skin golden in the sun. Her figure was rounder, fuller in the hips and bust.

"Isn't that the plan?" Pauline continued. "We'll pick up the gold before Sam Blade gets his dirty hands on it, then circle back to Hell's Picket and get to the bank so I can save our ranch." She stood with one hand on her hip.

"Yeah," Fargo said, trying to sound enthusiastic. "That's the plan." Nothing was going right. He'd failed to save the family, and now with Pauline along, she was in danger too. As soon as Sam Blade and his gang ran down Dena and the MacKenzie clan, they'd be heading for the gold. And as soon as they got their hands on that, Blade and his men would disappear, all of them wealthy men. Meanwhile, Pauline would still have lost her ranch to the bank. Fargo swore again under his breath. No, he decided. Pauline MacKenzie might well have lost her family, but at least she was going to get to save her property. It was the least he could do. He felt the rage swell in him as he thought of Sam Blade's tall figure, his cruel laugh, and how he'd nearly got him hanged back in Hell's

Picket. No, Fargo thought, Sam Blade was not going to get away with this.

"I'm going to get that gold," Fargo said, "if it's the last thing I do."

"Atta boy," Pete said approvingly. "We'll be nearly there by nightfall. Head due west to Hidden Canyon. That's what I call it, anyway."

As the sun neared its zenith, they mounted again and took off, Pete in the lead. They entered the cool shade of the woods and climbed up through fragrant ponderosa pines. Fargo glanced back over the yellow grass plain, but there was still no sign of pursuit. Where the hell was Sam Blade now?

Throughout the long afternoon Pete led on through dense forests, around the bases of huge buttes, and over low saddles between the scrub hills. Once they crossed a wide wagon track, two parallel grooves in a meadow, the trail overgrown with tall grasses.

"The Old Gap Trail," Fargo muttered, recognizing the track some homesteaders used before the Oregon Trail, further south, became so well-established.

They rode fast, not even trying to disguise their trail. Since Sam Blade had the map to the gold and would figure out they were heading there anyway, speed was all that mattered. As the sun slowly lowered in the west, they had climbed up to the high country again. Pete led them along a high ridge, and the forested land lay below them. The air was cooler, a dry wind blew, and piles of white cumulus clouds moved majestically across the deep blue sky. Lodgepole pines stood like tall sentinels, and scrub oak blanketed the ground. Pauline leaned her head against Fargo's back.

"You tired?" he asked her.

She nodded and tightened her arms around him. He could tell by the way she leaned against him that the strain was beginning to take its toll on her—the death of Mack, the murder of her son, being separated from her children, and now being hunted by a gang of roughs. It was amazing she'd held up as well as she had. He felt the softness of her breasts against his back and the firmness of her thighs pressed against his legs. He thought of Dena, Julie, and the two young children. Sam Blade and his men were desperados of the worst kind, and he knew they would stop at nothing, not even the murder of innocent children to get what they wanted. He put the thought out of his mind and concentrated on the trail ahead. There was nothing a man could do about the past. He just had to face the future.

As the sun touched on the distant peak, Pete reined in his Appaloosa, and the Ovaro came to a halt beside Fargo. They sat looking down over an immense wild green forested tract bordered by high, rocky snow-capped peaks. Here and there was the silver glint of a river. The forest was cut with deep rocky gorges and blind canyons, all choked with the dense black green of the pines. From here Fargo could see that the land below could swallow a man forever.

"Sutter's gold is right down there," Pete said, pointing downward. "But if you didn't know it, it would take you a hundred years to find it. I just got lucky and stumbled on it one day when I was hunting."

As they watched, the last golden light of the sun grew rosy, and the shadows of the peaks grew long across the thick forest. Fargo felt tiredness overwhelm him. There was no way they could push on tonight. After a good sleep they'd be ready for Hidden Canyon in the morning. He looked around for a campsite and spotted a sheltering cliff at one end of the ridge. From here they could keep an eye on the land below. They couldn't risk having a fire, so it would be a cold night. There was no telling where Sam Blade and his men could be now.

Pete's shoulder was sore, but he was managing all right. He watered the horses at a fresh spring just down the hill, as Fargo spread out their blankets. Then the three of them sat silently, huddled in their blankets against the cliff, as the sky faded from blue to black and the stars came out one by one. They chewed pemmican and dried berries for supper.

"I'll take the first watch," Fargo said. He put on an extra flannel shirt against the cool mountain air and donned his buckskin jacket. He checked the bullets in his Colt and left them. For the first few hours he stood by the rocks, looking out at the night. All was still except for the occasional flutter and call of the hunting owls. The moon rose steadily and then began its descent. He scanned the land below all the way to the distant horizon for any sign of a campfire. All was dark. But it was possible that somewhere, out there, Sam Blade and his gang were sleeping, as they were, without a fire.

Fargo decided to walk down to the stream for a drink of water before waking Pete to take over. As he neared the babbling water, he saw a movement in the trees. It was not an animal. Of that, he was certain. It had been a man, a silent dark form. Fargo thought immediately of Ponca.

He knelt down and took a drink as if he hadn't noticed anything. Then he quickly turned and walked back up the hill. The moon was slipping up over the horizon. Once out of sight, he doubled back, making a wide loop into the wooded slope, slipping silently among the trunks of the trees. His keen eyes were alert for any motion, his ears sensitive to every sound. When he neared the brook, he paused and then saw the form of the man disappearing through the woods. He'd catch Ponca this time. Keeping the dim, moving shadow just in sight, Fargo followed on silent feet through the trees. He was gaining on the Indian now, trying to get close before Ponca could jump on the horse he undoubtedly had hidden nearby.

Ahead in the forest were ghostly shapes of huge rocks, big as houses, and pale in the light of the rising moon. The Indian headed toward them. Fargo grew wary and silently pulled the Colt from his holster. Ponca disappeared between two of the rocks, and Fargo angled to one side. This was the perfect place for an ambush, he thought, if the scout suspected he was being followed. Fargo eased silently around the back of a huge boulder, expecting to see the Indian crouching there, waiting to jump him. But there was no one.

Fargo stood for a moment, listening to the sounds of the night—the waiting silence, the moan of wind in the pines. And then there came a whisper of noise. Fargo had just enough time to raise his arms above his head as the Indian came down full force on him from the top of the boulder.

He felt the Colt fly out of his hand. Moonlight flashed on the long lethal blade of a knife, aimed at his throat. Fargo brought his right up hard, and his powerful grip caught the man's wrist just in time. The knife blade trembled, nearer and nearer, as he poured all his strength into his arm. The Indian was strong as a cougar. The knife wavered nearer Fargo's neck, and he felt the coolness as the metal blade nicked his skin. Slowly, slowly, he willed his powerful muscles, and the knife slowly rose through the air.

They stared at one another eye to eye, the Indian's face dark, an expressionless mask in the moonlight. A thought flashed through Fargo's mind—this Indian was bigger than the figure he'd seen by the lake.

Suddenly, the man jerked away and leapt to his feet. Fargo crouched, his hands before him. He eyed his Colt lying on the ground just six feet away. Could he dive for it? With a silence more terrifying than a war cry, the Indian sprang forward again, his knife whistling through the air. Fargo moved aside just in time before it sliced through his shoulder. He caught the Indian off balance, kicked out at his leg, and drove into him, knocking him off his feet.

Fargo went down on top of him, and they rolled over and over on the ground, ending up with Fargo on top. His iron grip held the Indian's powerful knife arm, which he smashed again and again against the hard-packed ground until the knife fell away. He held the Indian pinioned. The man's dark eyes glittered in the dappled moonlight.

"You kill me?" the Indian asked. Fargo was surprised to hear him speak English.

"That depends," Fargo said. "What's your name?"

"Wolf Shadow," he replied.

Fargo regarded him for a moment. "Shoshoni?"

"From the north."

"Why did you jump me?" Fargo asked.

"Why were you following me?" Wolf Shadow said.

"Fair question." Fargo laughed. "I thought you were a man named Ponca."

At the sound of the name Wolf Shadow started. "This Ponca . . . he is . . . your friend?" the Indian asked, hesitatingly.

"My enemy," Fargo said.

"Then we have same enemy," Wolf Shadow replied. "I am also hunting Ponca."

Fargo knew the Indian was telling the truth. He stood slowly and retrieved his gun, then handed the knife back to Wolf Shadow, who slipped it into his scabbard.

"I am the Trailsman," Fargo said then. "White

men call me Skye Fargo. But long ago your tribe called me Runs-With-Buffalo."

"I have heard many stories about you," Wolf Shadow said with a broad smile. "Come, we will sit by a fire and tell many stories tonight."

"No. I am traveling with two friends," Fargo said. "They're sleeping up on the ridge." Suddenly, he grew concerned. He'd been gone half an hour, and he was supposed to be keeping watch. "I need to get back."

As they hurried back through the black forest, they spoke in quiet voices, exchanging stories. Wolf Shadow told Fargo that Ponca had come north to his tribe the year before and tried to join up with them. But Ponca had been a trouble-maker from the start, stealing one man's squaw and another man's horses. Finally, the tribe had expelled him, and he tried to kill the chief unsuccessfully. Wolf Shadow had been sent to hunt him down and bring him back to the Shoshoni tribe for punishment.

They reached the cliff and found Pete standing guard with his rifle. He raised it when he caught sight of Wolf Shadow, but Fargo assured him everything was all right.

"I got worried when you didn't come wake me," Pete said. "I'll take over the watch now. You get some rest, Fargo." Wolf Shadow decided to stand guard with Pete, and Fargo moved toward his bedroll. Pauline was fast asleep. Just as he was about to lie down, she began tossing and turning, calling out in her sleep incoherently. Fargo knelt down beside her and shook her shoulder gently.

She opened her eyes and gasped, started to cry out, and then realized who he was. She clung to him, and the tears on her cheeks glittered in the moonlight.

"You're all right now," he said, his arm around her. "You were having a bad dream."

"I know," Pauline said. "Please, Skye, just hold me."

Fargo lay down beside her, and she nestled in the crook of his arm. They fit together like two spoons, and somehow, Fargo thought, it felt natural to hold her after their long day in the saddle together. Her body's soft curves felt familiar to him as he rested his arm around her, holding her close and inhaling the scent of her hair, which made him feel slightly dizzy.

"When will we ever be safe again?" Pauline murmured. "And Julie, and Jimmy, and Hanna— do you think they're all right in Hell's Picket?"

Fargo heard the doubt in her voice. And he knew that she guessed something had gone wrong with their plan. But he couldn't bring himself to tell her the truth—that if Sam Blade's men had caught up with her children, they were dead for sure. And that it was all his fault—he'd figured it out wrong. The silence lengthened between them.

"I'm sure they're fine," he said. "If anybody could get them to safety, it's Deadeye Dena. They're tucked in safe in the Hell's Picket Hotel right now. That's for sure, so don't you worry."

"Thank you," Pauline said. He heard in her voice that she didn't believe him, that she knew he was trying to fool himself too. He held her tight, thinking how short life could seem sometimes, how precious every moment was. How you never knew what the next minute was going to bring, joy or sorrow.

Pauline laid her hand over his as lightly as a bird on a branch. She stroked it gently and pressed her soft rear against him. He found himself nuzzling her hair, hungrily, breathing in her scent. She moved his hand to cup her soft breast. And then it happened slowly and silently, almost as if they had done it many times before. Some part of him felt as if he already knew Pauline, and it seemed the most natural thing when she turned to lie on her back and he hovered over her, then kissed her deeply, enjoying the sweet warmth of her mouth, exploring it with his tongue, as she began unbuttoning her shirt.

5

With one fingertip Fargo traced the dark line of Pauline's arched brow as she slowly unbuttoned her shirt. He slipped his hand inside and cupped the soft fullness of her, the nipple a hard button between his fingers. She opened her shirt, and he saw her tawny breasts washed with moonlight, the dark nipples surrounded by a dark areola. He bent over and took the nipple in his mouth, tongueing her.

"Mmmm," she purred, her fingers winding in his hair, tickling his ears. "Yes, please, Skye. Just make me feel safe. Just for tonight."

Fargo darted his tongue across to her other nipple, then slowly made his way down her slender rib cage. She unbuttoned her skirt and pulled it down across her rounded belly. He continued downward, exploring, one hand covering her breast, the other helping her inch down her skirt.

Her skin was deliciously soft and her natural perfume musky and heavy. Enough to make a man drunk on her, he thought, trailing his tongue down across her belly, toward the dark tangle of fur between her legs. His hand inched upward along her smooth thigh as she shivered and purred again. His fingers found her wet and steaming, and he slowly inserted them into her dark cave, feeling her heat ready for him. He felt his swollen cock throbbing to be inside her, and then she pushed him away gently and spun around so that her head was between his thighs. She began to unbutton his Levi's, slowly, and pulled them off him.

Fargo pushed her thighs apart and nuzzled her as he felt her cool hand slip around his hardness, then the warmth of her mouth, her sucking tongue taking him inside her fully as he drank her in, exploring the sweet musky folds of her, breathing her in.

"Oh, yes, yes, darling, yes," she murmured, her back arching in ecstasy.

Her mouth swirled around his huge throbbing hardness, her tongue flicking the tip and all along the shaft as waves of pleasure coursed through him. Back and forth, she moved, sucking, caressing, stroking, in and out of her warm mouth. He darted his tongue into her, and she moaned, moved her rounded hips up and down, faster and faster. Suddenly, he could hold back no longer.

He pulled her around, and she came open to him as he plunged deep inside her, his cock throbbing with the sensations of her soft firmness welcoming him in. She hooked her legs around his waist as he rode her, driving deeper and deeper, as she pushed upward.

"Yes, yes, I'm coming—now, now," she whispered.

He felt himself give way as she came up to meet him, their bodies locked together in excruciating pleasure, the contractions again and again, as he came in her, pumping up harder, deeper, and she tightened around him.

"Yes, yes," she murmured.

The climax seemed to last forever, whirling the stars around in the sky as he shot into her hot tunnel, filling her up, spurting, hot, again and again, feeling the release of everything, her fever-ish soft body beneath him, her arms holding him. Finally, he slowed and gently lay down on top of her, nose to nose.

"All right?" he murmured.

"Ummmm, yes. Safe."

She smiled up at him, and he saw the sadness in her eyes, the fear for her children's safety, the trauma she had been through. She'd had a mo-ment of forgetting all that—they both had—but it had only been a moment.

Fargo lay beside her and cradled her next to him beneath the blanket. He was tired, but sleep did not come easy.

When first light came, Fargo rose and dressed. After washing at the stream, he found Pete and Wolf Shadow standing at the edge of the ridge.

"See anything?" he asked.

In answer, Pete pointed to the horizon, to the right of the rising sun. Against the robin's egg blue sky, he saw a faint yellow stain. It was barely visi-ble, and most men would have missed it. But Pete and Wolf Shadow both knew the signs of the wild country. What they both saw there was the smoke of a campfire—a fire that had been put out some-time before light came. But the last of the smoke was still rising and being dissipated in the light wind.

"I make it about forty miles," Fargo said. Wolf Shadow nodded agreement. "A day's ride in this rugged country."

"It's time we get on down to Hidden Canyon," Pete said. "We can be there in an hour."

In ten minutes they had packed everything and watered the horses down by the stream. Pauline washed up, then gave Fargo a kiss as he helped her mount the Ovaro. Pete chuckled and looked away. Wolf Shadow fetched his jet black horse from where it had been hidden in a coulee. They rode out, Pete in the lead, descending the steep slope into the thick fir forest. In several minutes they encountered thick underbrush, high walls of rock, and sudden abysses that appeared in their path. Several times Pete started one way, only to discover they had to retrace their steps. The coun-try was deep cut with roaring streams and crum-bling cliffs, all overgrown with fall fir and thick tangled shadberry. They could go no faster than a walk, the horses picking their slow way along the steep slopes and through the tangled brush.

An hour later, they were riding beside a stream in a shadowy box canyon choked with willows and sumacs. The steep rock walls of crumbling gray stone loomed above them, and high up, along the rim of the canyon, was a fringe of dark pines that seemed to filter out the sunlight. Fargo kept look-ing upward, expecting to see someone—Ponca or

Blade's gang—standing up there looking down on them. But he didn't spot anything moving.

"Here!" Pete said triumphantly at last. "Right here." He pointed straight ahead into a dense thicket of sumac and chokecherry that climbed up a slope. "It was winter first time I found this place. Otherwise, I'd have never spotted it."

Pete jumped down off his horse. He stooped and examined the ground all around.

"Nope," he said. "We're the first ones here. There's only one way into this canyon far as I know." He began pushing his way into the thicket. Fargo and Pauline followed. Wolf Shadow hung back, uneasy.

In a moment they were surrounded by thick green branches. The ground under their feet was oozing with water, a spring bubbling up. That accounted for the thick vegetation, Fargo realized. There was nothing to be seen but the green leaves and tangled branches. Then, suddenly, Fargo saw ahead a huge stone archway that cut through the cliff, completely hidden by the trees. He led Pauline and the Ovaro through it and emerged in an egg-shaped canyon. Before him was the strangest place he had ever seen.

At the far end was a long waterfall, a silvery ribbon glistening against the steep gray rockface that encircled the entire canyon. The canyon floor was open and grassy. The scenery was unspoiled and silent, almost like the Garden of Eden. Except that in the center stood the grisly shapes of three burned-out wagons, charred slats and arches of the ribs that held the canvas covers still intact.

Pauline gasped and turned away. Fargo dropped the reins of the Ovaro and walked forward for a closer look.

Dozens of skeletons, picked clean by the buzzards and bleached by the sun, lay scattered all around, some with the tatters of Army uniforms still clinging to the bones. Some of the bony fingers were still wrapped around rifles and long Army knives half buried in the grass. Between the teeth of a grinning skeleton a purple-headed thistle had grown up. Bones littered the ground everywhere. Fargo shook his head at the carnage and the waste of human lives. Dozens of living men had been driven mad by greed, mad enough for some of them to plot to kill the others and run off with the gold. And in this otherwise beautiful canyon, they had fought each other to the death, every last one of them.

"It's really something, ain't it?" Pete asked somberly, coming to stand beside Fargo. Pauline still stood in the archway, unwilling to look at the gruesome scene. "I couldn't figure out what had happened when I first found 'em. But then I spotted the gold."

Pete motioned for Fargo to follow him. They stepped among the bones and rifles and knives. One skeleton lay beside a brass-framed tintype, the face long faded to blankness by the sun. They walked toward the wagons, and Fargo had a look inside. They were all empty, until they reached the last one. There he spotted the tatters of burned fabric, like heavy canvas. Enough of it had burned away that he could see a small pile of what looked like ruddy pebbles inside. Fargo picked up one of them and bit it, then looked at the tooth marks. They glistened gold.

"That's right," Pete said. "Gold shot, high-grade. And this is just a little of it. There's a cave too." He dug in his pockets and handed Fargo a couple of pieces of short candles, then led him toward the waterfall that cascaded into a deep pool. Fargo looked around for an outlet, but saw no stream. Clearly, the water just soaked back into the earth and bubbled up again, maybe some of it in the spring at the mouth of the canyon. Pete led him along the edge of the pool. Fargo didn't see any entrance to a cave. Then Pete suddenly stepped behind a rock and disappeared. Fargo followed through a narrow cleft and found himself in a shallow cave. It was so small that the reflected light made it possible to see. Fargo pocketed the candles. There on the floor was a huge pile of canvas bags. It was a fortune in gold. A ton at least. Fargo whistled.

"Some of them were hiding it in this cave," Fargo surmised. "And they got surprised by the others." He stood looking at the pile and realized they had a big problem. There was no way they could pack all this gold out of the canyon on two horses and still run fast enough to stay ahead of Sam Blade and his men. They could take away enough gold for Pauline to pay off the bank note on the ranch and leave the rest for Sam Blade. Fargo gritted his teeth. The idea of that low-down son of a bitch getting away with murder and getting rich to boot was unbearable. No, there had to be a way to foil him. And they had only a few hours to come up with something.

Fargo considered an ambush. But there were too few of them to take on Sam Blade's whole gang. If they could just hide the gold before Blade and his men arrived. Then they could ride off to Hell's Picket with Blade in hot pursuit, assuming they had the gold. That would lure him all the way back to town where, with Pauline's testimony, Sheriff Sikes might finally see reason. But then Fargo remembered that the whole posse was off chasing their tail led in the wrong direction by Ponca. Sam Blade had said so himself. And with the ten nasties in his gang, Blade could easily out-gun the able-bodied men left in Hell's Picket. There'd be a bloodbath. Still, the minutes were ticking away, and every passing moment brought Sam Blade and his men nearer to Hidden Canyon. Fargo made up his mind in a flash.

"We're going to haul this gold out of the cave and drop it in the pool," Fargo said. "Then we're going to get the hell out of here and lead them on a wild-goose chase. At some point we'll run across help. And some time later, we'll come back and fish that gold out of the pond."

"Sam Blade will sure be surprised when he arrives and finds a fortune in bones," Pete said, chuckling.

Pete and Pauline stood watch at the entrance to the canyon while Fargo and Wolf Shadow set to work. The canvas bags were sewn shut securely, but they were damned heavy and awkward to move, hard to get a grip on. Finally, they managed to drag the first one across the floor of the shallow cave and to the rocks at the edge of the pond. They hoisted it over and let it go with a splash. It billowed for an instant, then sank quickly, a stream of bubbles trailing upward. At first Fargo feared that the bags could be seen from above, but the canvas blended into the rocks deep in the water, and the waterfall made ripples, making it impossible to see clearly. Wolf Shadow shook his head as he looked down into the water.

"I don't understand white man's love for this yellow metal," he said sadly.

"Yeah," Fargo said. "A lot of white men would kill us for this." He turned back to the cave. There were nine more bags. For the next two hours they struggled with hiding the gold. It was not an easy job. As the sun rose higher, Fargo became more and more impatient. The one thing he didn't want was to get trapped in this blind canyon by Sam Blade's gang. They needed to finish the job and get the hell out. Finally, it was done, the last bag sent into the water. The submerged canvas bags had almost stopped bubbling and, unless you knew, you'd never guess they were there. Fargo tied up the small pile from the wagon and stowed it in his saddlebag.

Wolf Shadow went to guard the entrance while Fargo and Pete brushed away all the tracks around the cave entrance and on the cave floor while Pauline got the horses saddled and bridled. All was ready. Fargo felt an immense sense of relief. For all its beauty, Hidden Canyon was a creepy place, a place that almost made you believe in evil spirits.

Just then, Fargo heard a faint cry. He felt the hair rise on the back of his neck as all his senses became immediately alert. He raced toward the archway, Colt in hand. Pete followed with his rifle. He slowed and peered out from behind a rock into the dense greenery. He saw a motion, low down, and he aimed his Colt, finger tight on the trigger. Then he recognized the form of a man, dragging himself across the sodden ground through the underbrush. It was Wolf Shadow. Blood drenched his back, soaking through his buckskins.

"Cover me," Fargo said to Pete. He dashed forward and pulled Wolf Shadow through the archway, past the sheltering rocks. He propped him up and saw immediately that he was done for. His belly had been ripped wide open with a knife. His hands were slashed too. It had been a fast fight and a vicious one. Wolf Shadow's eyes were focused far away.

Wolf Shadow's lips moved silently. Fargo leaned closer as his lips moved again. "Ponca," he whispered. His eyes went dull.

"Let's go," Fargo said. "Now."

Pete motioned to Pauline to bring up the two horses. She gasped when she saw Wolf Shadow. Pete handed her a pistol, and she gripped it, her eyes suddenly flashing. Fargo went out first, on foot, pushing warily through the thicket. His Colt was at the ready, every nerve stripped raw, expecting at any moment for Ponca to leap out at him, knife whistling. But he emerged from the thicket and looked around at the shadowy box canyon rimmed with tall trees. There was no one in sight. Fargo told Pete and Pauline to remain behind in the cover of the thicket. He eased forward, stepping out, his body tense and ready. His sharp eyes found the prints in the soggy ground. Two men in moccasins, fighting, blood on the ground. Fargo's eyes followed the smaller man's prints as they ran away from the fight. He followed for thirty yards. There were droplets of blood on the ground. So, Ponca was wounded too. Fargo's hopes rose as he saw from the unevenness of the tracks that the Indian was limping and limping bad.

Fargo's keen eyes swept the ground and the trees around him. Just ahead, he saw the tracks veer off into a stand of pines. On the bark of the tree was a bloody handprint. He circled around the grove, feeling certain Ponca had climbed one of the trees and was waiting in the thick-needled branches, to jump him, the desperate act of a wounded man.

Suddenly, there was a rustle of sound behind him. In a flash Fargo realized Ponca had played his last trick card. He'd left the bloody handprint on purpose. Fargo whirled about as the Indian rushed out from behind a rock, his long knife singing in the air. Fargo kicked out at Ponca's knife, catching the Indian's hand with his boot, and the knife flew upward. The Indian hit him full force, smashing his hand against a rock. The Colt fell on the ground, and they rolled over and over in the dirt, struggling for a grip on one another. Ponca was wiry and damned strong, his muscles like bands of iron. His eyes were like those of a weasel, small and glitteringly cruel in his swarthy face. But he was wounded, blood darkening the front of his buckskins. Fargo delivered a hard uppercut that snapped back Ponca's head, then a left to the gut. The Indian sagged, then seemed to come back to life with a relentless fury, scratching and biting and lashing out, squirming under him. Then, suddenly, Ponca's hand reached out and came up with Fargo's Colt. Fargo gripped the Indian's wrist as it tried to point the gun at his head and forced it backward. The energy flowed into Fargo's powerful shoulder and arm as, inch by inch, the Colt was lowered until the barrel was pointing straight at Ponca's head. The Indian was beat and he knew it. His unreadable black eyes locked onto Fargo's, and he grimaced. Then Ponca's finger pulled the trigger.

The bullet tore through Ponca's skull. Fargo got up and retrieved the bloody weapon, wiping it clean on the dead Indian's leggings. Wolf Shadow and his tribe were avenged. Ponca had got his just rewards. And now, with Ponca dead, Sam Blade had lost a damned good scout, Fargo knew. It just might give them the advantage they needed to get away. Without Ponca tracking them, it would be much easier to mislead Blade's gang.

Fargo ran back toward the thicket and gave them the all-clear signal. Pauline and Pete emerged, and they mounted the two horses, Pauline behind Fargo.

"I'm scared," she said.

"Just keep your pistol ready," he said. "We might

have to shoot our way out." Her arm was tight around his waist.

"Which way out?" he called to Pete.

"Not the way we came," Pete said. "That's the route they'll be following on the map."

Pete led the way up the shadowy box canyon. Once again, Fargo glanced around, uneasy, at the dark trees that lined the rim of the canyon. As they rode, the winding canyon became narrower and shallower with fewer trees. They had gone a mile when Fargo glimpsed up ahead a gradual slope of scree. They could lead the horses straight out of the canyon and make their escape.

Then he heard the sound of jangling bridles and men's voices. He cursed. Because of the echo off the canyon walls, it was impossible to tell how close they were. And there was no place to hide in the narrow canyon. Pete came to a halt, listening too. And then Fargo caught sight of figures, men on horseback, at the top of the scree slope. There would be no escaping this way. He pulled the Ovaro around fast and headed behind a boulder, hoping they hadn't been spotted. His hopes were in vain. From behind came the sounds of gunfire. They'd been seen. The chase was on.

The Ovaro and the Appaloosa galloped back down the canyon as it deepened again and became more and more choked with trees. Fargo kept his eyes open for any side canyon where they might escape, but there were none. None except Hidden Canyon. They galloped past the green thicket. He was damned if he was going to get trapped in there. No, they had to keep going and going fast.

Fargo heard the sound of gunfire behind them, then it ceased, but he knew it was only because Blade and his men weren't wasting their bullets.

The trees went flying by as the canyon grew deeper and wider, the gray stone walls taller and taller. Soon they could come out into the forest valley, and from there they could climb the ridge and make their escape. Just as they rounded the last curve of the canyon, Fargo pulled up short. Pauline screamed. There, in a long line across the mouth of the canyon, were ten of Blade's men, sitting on their horses, rifles at the ready. Sam Blade sat off to one side on his horse.

"Goddamn," Fargo muttered. It had been a trap. A goddamn trap with Ponca sent in as bait. Sam Blade and his men had managed to plug up both ends of the canyon, and there had never been any chance of them getting away. As soon as they spotted the horses, Sam Blade's men gave a roar and pulled up their rifles. Fargo, Pete, and Pauline sat facing a line of rifle barrels, all aimed right at them. One move and the bullets would be thicker than mosquitoes in a swamp. There was a long silence.

Fargo knew there was no escape. If they turned and ran, they'd be shot in the back. Or if they managed to get away, they'd run smack into the arms of the rest of Blade's gang. For a moment Fargo considered shooting Blade. His trigger finger itched. But then he realized it would be suicide. Sam Blade had beat 'em all right, damn him. At least for the moment. There was every possibility they'd die, Fargo thought. All Blade had to do was to give the word. Now he had everything he'd wanted. Or almost. Pounding hooves and the jangle of spurs signaled the rest of Blade's men come riding down the canyon behind them. They were now completely surrounded.

"Let her ride out of here," Fargo said, "and Pete and I'll come with you."

"Ha! Or else what?" Sam Blade called back tauntingly. "I don't have to bargain with you, Mr. Trailsman. Now, throw down your guns, nice and slow."

Fargo hesitated, then saw there was no choice. He reluctantly threw his Colt down on the ground, followed by his Henry rifle. Pete did the same with his firearms. Pauline, the pistol in her hand, suddenly stiffened, and he knew she was about to try something.

"Throw it down," Fargo said softly. "We haven't got a hope in hell right now. We'll just look for a chance to get away."

"I'm scared, Skye," she whispered as she tossed the gun down to the ground.

"I'm right here," he said. But he knew they were only words. Sam Blade and his men were capable of cold-blooded murder, of rape, of even killing children. And now the three of them were completely in the gang's clutches.

"That's better," Sam Blade said. He spurred his horse and came riding up, his gun still ready before him, pointed straight at Fargo's chest. He removed his silver-banded black hat, and the sun glistened on his slick ebony hair. His huge chest and arm muscles strained at the dark fabric of his tight jacket. His piercing eyes ran over Fargo.

"I could shoot you dead right now," Sam Blade hissed. He tightened his finger on the trigger. Fargo felt Pauline, her arms around his waist, hold him tighter. "But nah. We were going to have us a nice hanging back in Hell's Picket. And I think that's what I'd like is a nice hanging. If you do it nice and gentle, it can be such a slow way to die," Sam Blade laughed.

Fargo started to answer, then realized he'd only antagonize Blade. No, he'd bide his time. Somehow, there'd be a way. Blade's men were moving in slowly like a pack of wolves.

"Nice to see you again, Miz MacKenzie," Blade said sarcastically. He peered at Yellow Pete. "And who might you be?"

Pete sat silently, his eyes flashing rage. He shook his gray head, refusing to answer.

"Why, he's that old drunk who came to the ranch," a gruff voice said. Fargo recognized Billy Guire's potbellied form and bald head.

"Oh," Sam Blade said quietly. "So you helped this son-of-a-bitch get those little wretches out of the house. And I bet you're the old man who drew this map too." Blade fumbled in his pocket and held up a folded piece of paper. He smiled. "I got a lot to thank you for, old man," he said. Sam Blade slowly pulled a rope from his saddle horn and began coiling it in his hands. Suddenly, he leaned forward and threw the rope in a lasso that snaked through the air and fell around Pete. Sam Blade jerked on the other end, and the rope instantly tightened around the old man's lean body. Sam Blade wound the end of the rope around his saddle horn.

"Let him loose," Pauline cried out.

"Say good-bye to your pals, you old drunken buzzard," Sam Blade called out. He dug his sharp roweled spurs into the sides of his horse, and it started forward. Pete was jerked off his horse. The old man hit the ground hard, being pulled after Blade's galloping mount. A wave of red fury rose up in front of Fargo, and with a hoarse cry he urged the Ovaro forward, following Blade. Pauline held on tight. In seconds the black-and-white pinto had pulled up alongside Blade's horse, and Fargo gathered his legs under him and then leapt sideways.

Sam Blade saw him coming, flying through the air, and his eyes opened wide. Fargo knocked Blade clear off his mount. They flew through the air, and Fargo saw the hard ground coming up. He hit with bone-jarring pain, right on his shoulder, his hands gripping Sam Blade. They rolled over and over, and in a blur Fargo saw Blade's horse come to a halt. The old man lay still. The red fury darkened to a black wall of rage.

To hell with it. He began pounding at Sam Blade. The big man lashed out; his powerful meaty arm delivered a right jab that caught Fargo under the chin. Then a hard right above the brow. Fargo felt his face split open, and the blood poured down his face. He responded with an uppercut that snapped back Blade's head. His eyes rolled up in their sockets, and Fargo pummeled

Sam Blade back and forth, until he thought the man's neck would break. Yes, Blade would pay for everything he'd done. Fargo would kill him if it was the last thing he did.

Then he felt rough hands seizing him, pulling him off Blade's inert body. He lashed out at the men, and through his blood-dimmed sight he saw them all gathered around him like buzzards at a kill. All ten of them, armed. And then they closed in. From a distance Fargo heard a woman scream, and he knew it was Pauline. With the butts of their rifles the gang pounded his back, his ribs, his legs. He heard the crunch of the bone in his ribs and his jaw as they kicked him. He tasted the dry dirt and the sting of salt, the warm silvery blood in his mouth. Agonizing lightning flashes of pain exploded along his limbs and through his spine. And then his body seemed to float away, as if the pain were coming from a long distance away. Then he heard a gruff voice say, "Leave him be. Let the boss finish him off." And he sank into waves of black nothingness.

He heard a woman sobbing. Red spots danced before his eyes. He tried to move, but it was impossible. The cries were quiet, desperate. He tried to speak, but he could not move his tongue. Every part of his body was heavy. He was sinking again into the dark waves.

Fargo forced his mind awake, forced himself to clench his jaw. He tried to clench his fists, but white hot pain shot up his right arm. The pain seemed to help him concentrate, so he clenched his fist again. His head cleared. Yes, he was alive. His eyes seemed glued shut, and he realized it was probably dried blood. He squeezed them hard until his tears ran and then blinked them open. It was nearly evening. He was lying, bound and gagged, on the ground beside a yellow campfire. Not far away, he spotted the shape of a charred wagon, and he knew he was in Hidden Canyon. He heard Pauline sob again, hopelessly and desperately. He saw her then, not far from him, lying on the ground, wrapped in blankets.

"Mmmmm," he said. The sobbing stopped immediately, and he repeated the sound.

"Fargo?" Pauline whispered. "You're alive!" She waited a moment, and he repeated the sound. "I'm all tied up, and I can't get loose," she said, her voice breaking. "Pete, they killed Pete." There was a moment of silence between them. "Blade's mad as hell. Oh, Fargo, I want to die now. I don't want to live through what they're going to do to us."

Fargo was lying there, listening to her voice. All the while he had been exploring the ropes that held him, wriggling his sore arms and legs, trying to find a weakness in the bonds. His head pounded with the pain, his tongue swollen, his eyesight dim and blurry. He'd been hurt bad, he realized. It hurt to breathe. It would take him weeks of rest to mend. That is, if he lived. Goddamn Sam Blade. Yes, the rope was loose. As he worked it back and forth, he thought he could feel it slipping on his wrist just a little bit. Yes, if he worked it long enough, he might just get one hand free.

He lay there, quietly working the rope, gathering strength in his mind. Pete dead. Wolf Shadow dead. MacKenzie and his son, Scotty, dead. And Julie and the kids probably dead too. And Deadeye Dena. All because of Sam Blade.

He'd lost track of time. He didn't know if he'd blacked out or fallen asleep, but, suddenly, there were a pair of boots standing in front of his face, and he was hauled to his feet. Night had fallen. There were campfires dotting the small canyon. A dark crowd of men stood around. Two men held him upright, one on either side. Pauline had been pulled to her feet. Her hair was wild, and her eyes were wide with fright. He caught her gaze and nodded. Her expression told him he must look like the living dead. Hell, he felt like it too, every muscle and bone in his body screaming in agony.

He heard someone approaching, and Sam Blade came to stand right in front of him. The man's face was full of hatred, his eyes shining with pure sadism. Suddenly, Sam Blade balled up his heavy fist and smashed it hard into his belly. Fargo felt his insides shift around and an agonizing flash of heat shooting along his ribs and up his back. Hell, he was a mess.

"Take off his gag," Sam Blade ordered. Fargo sucked on his swollen tongue and tried to lick his cracked lips.

"So, who's got the gold?" Sam Blade demanded. He turned and stopped and glared into his face. Fargo shrugged.

"Wasn't here when we got here," Fargo said. "I thought you'd already got it, Blade."

Sam balled up his fist again and delivered a right to Fargo's chin that made the two men holding him stagger backward. Stars danced before his eyes, and Fargo tasted the fresh flow of blood in his mouth. He fought to maintain his consciousness, his mind trying to slip away again into the dark, unfeeling waves. He didn't know how much more of this he could take before he blacked out again.

Pauline cried out. Fargo heard Sam Blade's boots heading toward the fire. He fought to open his eyes. When he did, he saw Sam Blade standing before him, waving a stick with a red-hot ember glowing at the tip. Blade brought it so close to his face Fargo could feel its heat.

"I could burn out one of your eyes, Fargo," Blade said. "Now, where's the gold?" Pauline sobbed. Fargo didn't blink, but looked steadily at Blade, memorizing every inch of the man's hateful face, a face that burned itself into Fargo's mind. Sam Blade moved the flaming brand forward.

"No!" Pauline sobbed. "No! Please. Please. I'll tell you."

Blade stepped backward and turned to look at her. He walked over toward her and tossed the brand aside. Then he started to pull up her dress.

"So, you're going to tell me where that gold is," Sam Blade said. "And I'm going to see just what you've got down here."

"It's in the pond," Fargo said, "under the waterfall."

His words fell heavily in the silence. Sam Blade slowly wheeled about.

"What was that, Fargo?"

"You heard me," Fargo said. "Under the waterfall. In canvas bags. A whole ton of gold, Sutter's gold. Enough gold to make every one of you a millionaire."

After another moment of startled silence, Fargo's words had the exact effect he had hoped for. One of the men stepped forward and seized a burning branch from the fire.

"Let's go take a look," he said. Sam Blade strode away from the fire, following the men who were crowding toward the waterfall. Billy Guire stayed behind to guard them.

"I'm sorry, Skye," Pauline whispered.

"It's okay. I told 'em," Fargo said. "Besides, they were going to find out eventually."

"Shut up," Guire spat. He pushed them to the ground again. With his feet and legs tied, it was impossible to get to his feet. Fargo lay still and worked furiously on the knotted ropes that held his wrists. Yes, they were loosening, but it would be hours before he could slip his hands free. Over by the falls he could see the fiery brands throwing flickering light on the waterfall and the stony cliff. The dark forms of Sam Blade and his gang gathered around the pond. Fargo heard a splash and wondered if Blade had made one of the men jump in. In another moment he heard laughter and cheering. Yes. Someone had probably dived down and spotted the bags.

Billy Guire stood looking in the direction of the falls, eager to see what was going on. Fargo swore as he tried to work his hands loose. He could feel the blisters on his skin where the rope was wearing. If only his hands were loose, this would be the perfect opportunity. But he was nowhere near getting free. Fargo cursed, then lay back and closed his eyes. He tried to relax his body while his hands continued to work against the ropes, twisting, easing, pushing apart, pulling, slipping.

He heard the excited voices of Blade's gang as they tried to figure out how to get the bags of gold hoisted out of the water. It wasn't going to be an easy job. The gold itself was heavy and the canvas bags hard to handle, especially if they were waterlogged. That would keep them busy and preoccupied for a while, Fargo thought. He hoped it would be long enough.

The men shouted and cheered over by the waterfall. There was more splashing. Somebody came running over, and Fargo heard the sound of bottles clanking. It sounded like the men were having a whiskey party. In another hour they were singing at the top of their lungs, all drunk. Fargo had managed to get one knot undone, and the ropes were getting looser. He could move one hand very well now and could almost get the wrist free. He thought about the Arkansas toothpick, the blade he usually kept in an ankle holster. Sheriff Sikes had confiscated it. Fargo thought longingly of its sharp blade.

After a few more hours Blade's gang staggered back toward the campfires, fumbling for their blankets. The big figure of Sam Blade strode into the circle of firelight, and he paused in front of Pauline's huddled form, then moved on. Fargo heard her whimper. They had to get away tonight. By tomorrow the men would be hungover and grouchy. The hoisting of the gold wouldn't go easily, and they'd be even more aggressive. Fargo could well imagine what they'd do to Pauline. Bill Guire threw an old horse blanket over Fargo, wrapped himself up in a blanket, and lay down on the other side of the fire, his pistol in his hand, his hat within arm's reach.

Fargo redoubled his efforts on the ropes and felt his hands swelling with the strain. He had to get free, he told himself. And suddenly, his hand slipped out of the rope. He breathed slowly and continued to work at the ropes until his other hand was loose. Quickly, he unwound the rope from around his arms, untying the knots. Then, beneath the blanket, he tugged at the knots that held his legs, and they too finally came free. Fargo glanced over at where Billy Guire lay snoring.

Slowly, very slowly, he eased himself along the ground until he was lying alongside Pauline. She was wide awake. She didn't make a sound as he began untying her hands from behind her back. In fifteen minutes she was free as well. They needed a gun—and a way out. And there was only one way—through the stone arch. But there was a guard posted there. Fargo had glimpsed a man earlier, walking back and forth at the one entrance to Hidden Canyon. He lay quietly for a moment, formulating his plan. Then he touched Pauline lightly on the shoulder and pointed to a rock beside the entrance to the canyon.

She nodded and rose silently, then moved like a

shadow among the sleeping men. Fargo held his breath. If anyone just happened to wake up . . . but after another moment she disappeared in the darkness, and Fargo knew she was waiting there by the rock.

He eased himself to his feet and was unprepared for the wave of dizziness that threatened to overwhelm him. The embers of the campfire spun around in his eyes. He was so stiff, it was an effort just to take one step, and every muscle and bone complained. Nevertheless, he took a step forward, ignoring the pain. He hooked somebody's thick sheepskin jacket off a tree branch where it was hanging and slipped into it. Near another man a dark hat sat on a low rock. Fargo took it also. He scanned around for a gun too, but the men all had them in hand. He'd wake somebody, lifting it. In another moment he was approaching the stone arch entrance, dressed in the sheepskin jacket, his hat brim low.

"My turn," he muttered to the man who stood slouched against the stone arch.

" 'Bout time you showed up," the other growled. The man walked off toward one of the campfires, and Fargo waited a few moments until the man had bedded down and probably dropped off to sleep. Then he signaled to Pauline, who emerged from behind the rock. Together, they walked underneath the stone arch. They were just about to plunge into the dense thicket when a voice came from their left.

"Stop. Who's there?" Fargo couldn't see the

man standing in the deep shadow under a thick pine. He thought fast.

"I've come to spell you," he mumbled. The man seemed to accept this, and he turned, then stopped and turned back, seeming to see that there were two people, not one. "What the . . . what the . . . ?"

Fargo didn't wait, but he moved forward in a leap and knocked the man sideways into the stone arch. His head cracked with a dull thud against the stone, and the man went down. Fargo seized Pauline's hand and moved forward into the thicket.

Overhead, the moon was descending the western sky. A cold mountain wind blew, whistling in the trees. They were on foot. But damn it, he was going to get them the hell out of here, he swore to himself. They moved quietly through the thicket, pulling aside the thick branches, slipping toward the open canyon. And that was when all hell broke loose.

6

As they eased forward through the dense brush, a deep voice spoke out of the darkness.

"Halt or I'll shoot."

Fargo jerked Pauline to one side as the gun spit fire just in front of them. The bullet whined and ricocheted off the rocks. The reaction was immediate. From directly in front of them, Fargo heard several men shout. Damn. He'd underestimated how many men Sam Blade had guarding the entrance. There were at least four in front of them, hidden in the density of the thicket. Another gun exploded just off to their left, and then another. They couldn't survive in the hail of bullets. Fargo pulled Pauline back.

"The prisoners!" one shouted. "At the entrance! They're trying to escape!"

Fargo and Pauline reluctantly retreated under the stone archway. Hoarse, confused cries came from inside the canyon as well. In a moment everyone would be awake. Maybe they could lose themselves in the hubbub. Fargo took off the hat he wore and jammed it onto Pauline's head, hoping that in the dark she'd pass unnoticed. Keeping close to the wall of the canyon, he hurried her around the perimeter of the campfires at a half run. Blade's men, still inebriated, were pulling on their gun belts and swearing. Men were running toward the entrance. Fargo pushed Pauline back behind some rocks as a group approached.

"That way!" Fargo called out in a raspy voice, motioning toward the entrance. "They're trying to get away."

The men hurried past. As Fargo ran by the line of hobbled horses, he automatically searched the darkness for the black-and-white pinto. But it wasn't there. So, it must have escaped when the men were trying to beat him to death in the shadowy box canyon. He was glad for that. The Ovaro should never belong to a man like Sam Blade.

Fargo pulled Pauline along, heading toward the waterfall. He had an idea. If they couldn't get out of the canyon, at least they could hide. So far, Sam Blade hadn't discovered the shallow cave. It would shelter them and maybe, just maybe, Blade would think they'd escaped after all and would go off looking for them.

Pain coursed along Fargo's limbs as they ran toward the waterfall. His head swam with dizziness as they edged around the pond, found the cleft in the rock, and slipped inside. Fargo lay down gratefully on the sandy floor of the cave, his head pounding again, his body aching everywhere. Pauline paced nervously back and forth. There wasn't much room in the semicircle cave, which had a pile of large stones to one side. From outside, they heard the cacophony of shouting and horses whinnying.

Fargo wondered what Sam Blade would make of their disappearance. It would seem they vanished into thin air. To the confused sounds of the gang's furious search, he let himself drift away into healing and forgetful sleep.

He awoke later to find Pauline beside him, wiping his face with a water-soaked handkerchief. It was cool, but stung in places. She lifted her cupped hand to his lips, and cold water dribbled into his dry mouth. It tasted heavenly. He came to full consciousness.

"Where did you get the water?" he asked.

"I poked my head outside. And there was no one there," she said. "So I filled this hat." Fargo sat up.

"You sure you weren't spotted?" he asked. She nodded, uncertain. "Thanks. But don't try it again. It's too risky." He took the handkerchief from her hand and finished mopping his face. "Let's conserve the rest for drinking," he added. There wasn't much left in the hat, and there was no telling how long they'd be waiting in the cave.

Fargo stood and for a half hour stretched his limbs and bent his joints, assessing the damage from the beating the day before. His face had several deep slashes, but they had already closed up with dried blood. A couple of ribs were broken—it hurt to breathe or to move his arms a certain way. And his jaw didn't seem to work properly. But other than that, his bones were miraculously intact. The worst part was the pain in his joints and muscles, the deep bruises. And his innards seemed shaken around as if there had been some damage within. He worked his body, slowly, painfully, gently stretching the muscles and tendons. Finally, he lay back down and slept another couple of hours.

When he awoke again, light was filtering in through the cave entrance. Pauline had fallen asleep beside him. She was curled up and breathing lightly. He heard men's voices close by—very close by. He eased himself toward the entrance and listened.

"They've got to be somewhere in this canyon!" It was Sam Blade's voice. "They didn't get past the guard. I want every inch of it searched. Every rock crevice, every tree, every inch of soil. They're here, and I want them found!"

Fargo swore inwardly. So, Sam Blade hadn't been misled into thinking they'd escaped the canyon after all. And Fargo knew it was only a matter of time before somebody got the bright idea to search the rock wall behind the pool. The cave entrance was hidden, but someone inching along the rock face would find it. And then the game would be up. Fargo rose and paced back and forth in the short cave. What to do now?

The air in the cave was cold, and he shivered as a draft blew across him. Then he stopped and turned as the realization hit him. A draft. Air. It was coming from the direction of the pile of rocks. Fargo knelt down and moved his hand slowly over the rocks, feeling the steady cold air blowing hard in and around them. That could mean only one thing—that this shallow cave was just the mouth of a much larger cave. Fargo immediately set to work. There was no time to lose. He bent to the task of silently removing the stones from the pile. It was slow work, and every motion was agonizing, as his arms and legs ached and pain inched along his nerves. Pauline woke with a start and sat up in the half light.

"What are you doing?" she asked.

Fargo put his finger to his lips. There might be men around, and the cave would amplify any noise they made. He signaled to her to help him, and she bent to the job of moving the smaller stones. After another hour Fargo could put his hand through a black hole in the rocks into nothingness. The air rushed faster now as they worked. Outside, Fargo heard men shout from time to time as the desperate search of the canyon continued. They had almost widened the hole enough when Fargo heard voices approaching. The men were very close. He paused, not wanting to move in case they heard him. Pauline froze, holding a heavy rock.

"How about that ledge back there?" a voice said. "Anybody search that?" There came the sounds of boots scraping along rock. Fargo took the rock from Pauline, then positioned himself to one side of the cave entrance. It was not a moment too soon. The cave darkened as a man's form slid in through the rock crevice. As soon as his head appeared, he looked around for an instant, his eyes adjusting to the gloom. Before he could call out, Fargo hit him over the skull with the rock. The man's head dropped, and his body sagged forward. Fargo pulled him inside the cave.

"Hey, Ed!" the voice called. "What'd you find?"

The voices outside the cave grew more agitated as they tried to figure out what had happened. The hubbub swelled, and more and more men collected in front of the pond, all arguing about who would go in next. Sam Blade arrived and began issuing orders.

Meanwhile, Fargo was wasting no time. They had to get into the larger cave now or be recaptured by Sam Blade. He knew the danger. He knew it was a desperate move. But he also knew what would happen to both of them if Blade recaptured them. Fargo pulled the rocks aside as the hole widened. He motioned to Pauline to try to squeeze in, and at the same moment he heard another man fumbling along the ledge at the entrance. Once again he waited, rock in hand. What he wouldn't give to have his Colt, he thought. A second head appeared, but this time the man was ready, gun in hand. Fargo hit him just as the man spotted Pauline kneeling by the hole between the stones. He pulled the trigger reflexively, and the bullet went wide, ricocheting around the tiny chamber. Fargo wedged the unconscious man's body into the narrow crevice and wrenched the pistol from his grip.

"Let's go," he said to Pauline as the men began shouting outside. It would only be a matter of moments before they sent in another man and more bullets. The next time they might not be so lucky. Pauline eased herself into the hole. It was a tight fit around her hips, and then she was gone. Fargo followed, wedging his broad shoulders between the stones. The wind was fierce inside, and it was absolutely pitch black. He could hear the sound of rushing water in the distance. That was good. If they followed it, maybe they would find an exit to the cave. He thought of the tinder box in his pocket and then remembered the stubs of candles he had put in his jacket the day before. They would have some light, anyway. But first they had to get away from the entrance. He groped in the blackness and found Pauline's hand. He moved forward inch by inch.

"Slide your feet along the floor," he said. His whisper splintered and echoed in a thousand voices. They moved down a slick rock slope for ten yards. Fargo had the sensation that they were entering a larger chamber and the walls were falling away from them. The wind lessened. When he looked behind him, he could see the faint glow of the cave entrance in the distance. He halted, pulled out the tinder box, and struck a light. Pauline gasped in fright. They stood at the very edge of a black, seemingly bottomless abyss. One more step and they would have plunged to their deaths. Fargo lit a candle. The puny light flickered over the complex forms of pale white stalactites that dripped from the ceiling and pillars of stalagmites growing up from the floor of the cave. Fargo spotted a ledge that ran around the gaping abyss. He led Pauline along it until they reached an archway and ducked inside.

Fargo blew out the candle just when a noise exploded from the direction of the cave entrance. The light there flickered. A boom resounded through the cavern, echoing again and again. Rotten stone broke away from the walls and showered down at the sound of the gunfire.

"You hear me, Fargo?" Sam Blade's voice reverberated. There was a long silence. Fargo decided not to answer. "Son-of-a-bitch," Blade muttered. "Where the hell are they?" Fargo listened carefully to the voice, calculating where Sam Blade was standing near the entrance. He raised the pistol in his hand and aimed at the spot, then pulled the trigger. Once again the cave boomed with the sound of a shot. Sam Blade screamed with rage and pain. Fargo smiled to himself. A lucky shot in the dark. Too bad he hadn't killed Blade. He wondered what part of Sam Blade's anatomy he'd hit and hoped for the worst. There was a flurry of movement as Blade retreated, screaming in pain. Then Fargo heard the sounds of men's voices again. And then, Blade's enraged shout.

"Good night, Fargo," he screamed. "I'm closing your grave!" There came a deafening roar. Fargo hastily lit the candle.

"Come on!" He urged Pauline along the narrow path downward.

"What's going on?"

"They're burying us alive," he said. Behind them the sound of gunfire continued, a steady firing again and again. And then the sound was replaced by a roar that grew deeper, heavier, and he felt the walls of the cavern tremble. It was the sound of tons of rotten rock falling. The entrance would be sealed. As they hastened downward, a cloud of dust overtook them and obscured their vision. Fargo slowed again, feeling the floor with his feet. They came to clearer air and entered another chamber, so large they could not see the far side by the light of the candle. In the center was an emerald green lake with a rippled shore that seemed to be made of white marble. But it was fine sand.

"Let's rest here," Fargo said. "We're out of danger for the moment."

He sat down against a rock and pulled her close. Then he blew out the candle. She shivered in the dark.

"Can't we keep it lit?"

"We don't have many hours of light," Fargo said. "We've got to conserve the candles we've got."

The darkness was so intense, it was like black velvet before his eyes. After a while his vision swam with orange figures and then blue flashing lights. The sound of dripping water was like the ticking of a clock.

"Are we going to live?" Pauline asked.

"The wind in this cave means there's another opening somewhere," Fargo said. "All we have to do is find it."

What he didn't tell her was that these caves sometimes twisted around for miles. And that even if they did find the exit, it might be blocked with a ton of stones that would have to be moved first. Or it might be a crevice between two huge boulders, too narrow for them ever to slip out of.

In all likelihood, they'd die in the cave. Pauline voiced his thoughts.

"I'd rather die in this cave," she said, "than in the hands of Sam Blade. Thanks for getting us away from him."

Fargo thought of what might have happened to them, particularly to Pauline, once Sam Blade had turned his attention back to them. Rape, torture, mutilation. Yes. The cave was better.

For a timeless time Fargo dozed, stretched out on the fine white sand. It was the best sleep he'd had in many days, certainly the longest. He came to consciousness again later, wondering if a day or two had passed. He stood up in the blackness, stretched, and felt the soreness in his limbs. It was less. The sleep had done him good. Pauline came awake and stood also.

"Can we have some light?" she asked.

"Every minute could mean the difference between life and death," he said. "Let's get some water and have a little bath." Fargo stripped off his clothes and heard Pauline doing the same. He left his clothes and the precious candles in a pile, then groped in the darkness for her hand and led her, feeling his way with his feet, down the slight slope of sand, until he felt the icy cold water touch his toes. He dropped her hand, waded in, then gasped. It was bone-chilling but refreshing. He felt the wounds sting, then go numb. He splashed water on his face and neck, then dunked himself completely and stood up. He waded out and heard Pauline splashing lightly at the shore.

"It's too cold for me," she said. "God, it's so

dark." He could hear more than just fear in her voice, but a kind of desperation for light.

"We're safe," he assured her. He found her in the darkness and drew her close. Her skin was warm in the cool air. He held her, enjoying the curves of her softness against him. He kissed her deeply, then pulled her up onto the bank again where they made love, slowly, gently. Anything to pass the time and to take her mind off what might come. Anything to make her feel safe. He ran his fingers lightly over her face, imagining what she looked like.

Afterward, they dressed and slept again for a few hours. Fargo searched his pockets. He had a handful of dried pemmican, but he decided he would save it as long as possible. It would be a good surprise when their spirits started to flag and the real hunger set in. He had plenty of tinder and flint as well as a small metal case of wooden matches. He counted the candles carefully—a medium-sized one and two short stubs. Probably seven hours of light all told.

Then Fargo thought about the enormity of the odds against them. They would spend most of their time wandering in this cavern in the pitch black, never knowing if the next step could plunge them down a cliff or lead them to safety. Luckily, they had plenty of water. And the air in the cavern seemed fine. But soon they would be hungry. And worse than that, dispirited.

It was time to move, time to plan and to try. Fargo decided first to retrace his steps and return to the cave. Maybe there would be a way out there. He stood up and pulled Pauline to her feet. Moving around would do them good. He was determined to go slowly and not to use the light unless absolutely necessary. He held Pauline's hand and stretched out the other, groping in the blackness ahead and above him for any projecting rocks. He shuffled forward, feeling the slope of the sand beneath his boots, then the firmness of the rock. He remembered the distance up the long tunnel and through the archway. It seemed to take hours as they inched their way along the ledge and then came to the large chamber at the entrance. The air was still heavy with the smoke of crushed stones. And the floor was rough with rubble.

Fargo knew he had to use one of the precious matches to look around. He groped his way across the rough rock until his hands reached a new rock slope, the result of the cave-in. He struck the match. The huge chamber was half filled with boulders and heavy rubble that had collapsed as a result of the gunfire and the loud noise. But it wasn't so much what he saw by the light of the flame that discouraged him. It was the flame itself. The bright golden light stood upright in the still air. He watched as it burned down to his fingers, then winked out, leaving a momentary red ember behind.

Fargo realized there was no wind passing through this end of the cave now. And that meant the collapse had been so complete that not even air could filter through the rocks. It would take more than his strength alone to move the tons of rock that now lay between them and the open air. They would have to find another way out.

Fargo said nothing as he headed downward again. The path was now familiar to his hands and feet. Pauline remained quiet, and he knew she guessed the gravity of their situation. When they felt the softness of the sand beneath their feet, Fargo suggested they rest. But Pauline said she was ready to press on. Then, suddenly, she tightened her grip on his hand.

"Look," she said. "Something. Some kind of light."

Fargo peered into the darkness, wondering if she was seeing things. But then he spotted it. A dull, watery glow. For a moment his hopes rose in him. But then the light seemed to move slowly, growing closer, then angling to one side.

"What is it?" Pauline whispered.

"A fish," Fargo said, "out in the lake. They make their own light." When they got hungry enough, he thought, that light would mean fresh fish—raw fish. Fargo remembered seeing by the light of the candle the shore line of the lake stretching away to the right. He decided to try that way. He led Pauline by the hand, feeling his way along the shore. They went on and on, sometimes finding the shore sandy and other times strewn with rocks, past smooth rock walls on the right that dripped with moisture.

He kept his ears open for the whirring sound of bats. That was always a good sign, since the creatures slept in the caverns and flew out each night to hunt. If they could find bats and follow them, it would be a way of finding the exit. But he heard nothing except the sound of rushing water ahead in the distance. It grew louder and louder, filling the space with a constant roar.

Suddenly, Fargo saw ahead of him another glow. He rubbed his eyes and looked again, thinking it was another of the phosphorescent fish. But the glow was larger, more diffuse, and didn't move. Fargo decided to risk another precious match. He struck it and held it aloft.

Now they were standing in a low space. The lake was deeper here, black instead of green. At one end it met a rock wall. And it had ripples on the surface. The match flickered out, and Fargo saw the image of its flame for a long time afterward. Then, slowly, his eyes adjusted to the darkness again, and the glow reappeared. Now he knew it came from the end of the lake. Maybe there was an outlet there. Fargo moved closer in that direction, remembering the shape of the shore he had seen in the brief light of the match. They had to climb over some rocks. And, finally, they came to the cold, dripping stone wall and could go no farther. The lake ended here. Fargo saw the glow more clearly than ever now. It was under water.

"Is it a way out of here?" Pauline asked.

"I hope so," Fargo said. "I'm going to dive in and see."

He gave the matches and candles to her for safekeeping, then stripped down to his shorts and started to wade in.

"Please be careful," Pauline said. He found her

and gave her a quick kiss. The water felt warmer here than in the other part of the lake. Fargo swam toward the dim light, his powerful arms taking long strokes in the water. Finally, as he neared, he saw that the light was filtering upward from underneath the water. Fargo took a deep breath and dived downward, opening his eyes and aiming for the light. There were large boulders, but here the light grew stronger. He tried to push himself through, but his lungs were burning, and he retreated, swam upward again, and emerged, gasping.

"Oh, Skye," Pauline called out. "You were down so long, I thought you were lost."

"There's a way out," he said. "But it's blocked by a huge rock. I'll try to move it out of the way."

He dove again, more sure now, knowing where he was going in the dimness. He headed for the largest rock and tried to ease it aside, but it didn't budge. Once again, he came up for air. Again and again he dove, sometimes moving the rock aside by inches. Other times, failing to do anything. Finally, he realized he was exhausted and could do no more. He swam back to shore, guided by Pauline's anxious voice, and hauled himself out of the water. His flesh was deathly cold, so she rubbed him with her skirt to get him dry and warm again. He dressed and lay down. Sleep came fast.

He awoke sometime later, then remembered what had happened. He sat up. The glow was gone. Had it been a dream? Then he laughed aloud for the first time in days. Pauline stirred beside him and woke up, listening to his laugh.

"What, Skye? What is it?"

"The light," he said. There was a long silence.

"It's gone," she said.

"It's night," he said, pulling her toward him and giving her a kiss. And Pauline laughed too, a laugh of relief, of hope. There was something suddenly very comforting about being able to tell when it was night and when it was day. They celebrated by eating some of the pemmican.

When the light reappeared, Fargo continued his diving. Today it went better. At last, he managed to force the big boulder aside and slip by it. Then he felt pulled upward by the air in his lungs. He glanced up and saw, between the protruding rocks, the silvery surface of water above him. And light. Yes, they could get out this way. His lungs were nearly bursting, his head reeling, but he pulled himself back into the darkness and came up sputtering and blind. He swam toward Pauline's voice, pulled himself onto shore, and lay for long moments, gasping.

"All right," he said at last. "Let's get out of here."

Pauline stripped down to her camisole and bloomers. Fargo tied their clothes into a bundle, secured by his belt. The passageway between the rocks was so narrow, he'd have to pull the bundle along behind him. They swam out together, and Pauline tried the dive, with Fargo right behind her. She seemed frightened of getting trapped between the rocks and was tentative. The first few times she barely made it to the big underwater boulder.

"You'll make it," he encouraged her. "Once you see where you're going down there."

Pauline took a deep breath and went under again. Fargo followed the dim form of her movement in the wavering light. This time she didn't stop, but squeezed past the boulder. He saw her start to panic as she ran out of air, so he pushed her upward as she pulled herself between the protruding rocks. Then, suddenly, she was free, and she rose, kicking. Fargo came up behind her, his lungs burning for oxygen. He burst up to the surface of the water, squinting in the morning sunlight. He gasped for air and dashed the water from his eyes. They had bobbed up in a deep pond in the middle of a canyon he did not recognize. Pauline sputtered and seemed about to go down again. Fargo pulled her to the bank, and they climbed out. Fargo dragged the bundle of their clothing out after them. After he caught his breath, he undid the belt and spread the wet clothes on the rocks, then lay back in the sun, exhausted.

"I can't believe we made it," Pauline said, wonderingly. "We're alive."

Fargo breathed in the air gratefully and felt the warmth of the sun on his skin. But his thoughts were on Sam Blade. There was no telling how many days they had been underground. Fargo examined his arms and legs. The bruises from his beating had faded to purple and even yellow in spots. Three days, he guessed. Maybe four.

By now, Blade's gang had probably retrieved the gold from the water and were making off with it.

Fargo knew the first thing he had to do was get Pauline back to safety. And then he would search for the missing Ovaro. Then, he told himself, he would hunt down Sam Blade and every last one of his men. It might take him years, but the revenge would be sweet. He noticed Pauline looking at him.

"Sam Blade," she said, reading his face. He nodded. She stood up and started to pull on her half-dry clothes. "Let's get going."

They hiked through the rocky canyon and across a ridge to a high meadow. Fargo took a sighting on the high peaks to the west and figured they were just north of where the trail entered the Old Gap country. They continued walking eastward as the sun rose toward midday.

Finally, they emerged, and Fargo recognized the big yellow grass plain. They would have to cross it to reach the hills on the far side and the trail that led southward to Hell's Picket. A half hour later, they were walking through the tall grass when Fargo heard the sound of gunfire behind them. Immediately, he dropped to his knees in the grass and pulled Pauline down alongside him. He rose slightly and peered backward in the direction they had come.

"Goddamn it," he muttered, disbelieving their bad luck.

Pouring down the grassy hillside were Sam Blade and his gang. One of the charred wagons bounced along behind them, obviously full of the gold. The men shouted with glee as they spotted Fargo and Pauline on foot and in the middle of the plain. There was no place to hide. Fargo saw Billy Guire riding way out in front, heading straight toward them.

Fargo looked around and noted a cutbank in the grasses. It was as good a place as any to make a last-ditch stand. They ran for it as the first bullets whizzed overhead. Fargo's hand itched for his Colt. The pistol stuck in his belt was useless for firing because of the dive underwater. It would take a day to dry out.

They scrambled to the cutbank and huddled at the base of it, Fargo covering Pauline with his body. This time it would be a fight to the finish, he knew. There would be no escape.

The sound of pounding hooves came over the rise, and Fargo saw Billy Guire galloping toward them, his pistol raised. Fargo jerked Pauline aside as Guire's gun exploded, and a bullet kicked up a fan of dirt where they had been an instant before. Fargo leapt to his feet as Guire whizzed by and caught hold of an edge of the saddle. He felt himself being dragged along by the horse as his strong biceps pulled him upward. Guire aimed the pistol at Fargo's head, but before he could fire, Fargo knocked the barrel aside, and the shot went wide. He grabbed the hot barrel and wrenched it from Guire's grasp, then spun it in the palm of his hand and fired upward. Guire's body jerked backward with the force of the bullet that caught him in the chest.

The horse reared back, screaming, and Fargo held onto the saddle as Guire fell heavily off the other side. Fargo grabbed the horn and pulled himself over, his toes searching for the stirrups as the horse came stamping back down to earth. Down the slope came the army of Blade's men. Fargo turned to face them down. One man against ten. The rage rose in him, darkening the sun and the yellow meadow. All he saw were the bright figures of the men he would kill. Bullets flew like hail around him, but he ignored them all. He took aim and fired.

The big man out front grabbed his torn chest, then rolled off his saddle and hit the ground. Fargo didn't stop, but fired again in quick succession, hitting the second man in the head. A third slumped down holding his gut. A fourth spouted from the neck like a red fountain. The fifth was knocked by the bullet's force that hit his side. All the while, Fargo guided the horse with his powerful thighs, occasionally reaching to jerk the reins. Back and forth, the horse danced across the plain.

The pistol clicked empty. Fargo swore and tossed it aside, pulling the rifle from the saddle scabbard. He felt searing pain along a thigh and knew he'd taken a bullet, but he ignored it. He pulled up the rifle and fired again, again, again, taking down three more of Sam Blade's men. The horse beneath him screamed and rose up, then took a staggering step forward. Fargo saw it had taken lead in the neck. Blood spouted. Fargo drove the horse forward, urging it toward the cutbank. The horse stumbled down the bank, shuddered, and sank to its knees. Fargo leapt off. His leg with the bullet wound collapsed under him. He crawled along the ground and pulled Pauline toward the shelter behind the hulk of the dead horse. He reloaded the rifle with bullets he found in the saddlebag. It was quiet for a moment, and Fargo knew that Blade's men were planning an all-out assault. It came in a moment. With blood-curdling yells the men suddenly appeared, rifles blazing, bullets raining in on them. The lead was so thick it was impossible for Fargo to get a clear shot. Pauline jerked and cried out.

"You all right?" he shouted over the firing.

"I think . . . my leg," she screamed. "I can't feel anything."

He glanced over. The wound was through the calf muscle. She wouldn't bleed to death immediately, he saw. The firing let up for a moment, and Fargo knew they were massing for another all-out assault. How long could he hold them off? An hour? Maybe two? He held the rifle, ready for the next assault. It came again, the men pouring over the hill, preceded by a hail of searing lead. Fargo fired, once, twice, again. Four men went down. Then five. Fargo blinked his eyes in disbelief. The line of attackers swept past, and the firing continued. He heard shouting. What was going on?

Fargo got to his feet, struggling against the numbness of his wounded thigh. He looked around. The plain was swarming with horsemen battling one another. Who the hell were they? What was going on? Suddenly, galloping across the grass, Fargo spotted a flash of black and white, a riderless horse. It was the Ovaro. Fargo pursed his lips and whistled. The pinto's ears pricked up, and it came about, looking for him. He whistled

154

again, and it galloped hard straight for him. With a string of bullets in one hand and the rifle in the other, Fargo leapt on the pinto's back.

All around him the battle raged. At one edge a lone figure galloped hell-bent up the grassy slope. Fargo recognized Sam Blade. The coward was trying to get away. And chasing him Fargo saw a small figure on a palomino. Fargo felt his hopes rise. Deadeye Dena! She was alive. He urged the Ovaro forward after them as they disappeared over the top of the rise. The pinto sped up the slope.

At the top he saw them just ahead. The powerful Ovaro was gaining on the two riders as they approached the edge of the woods. Sam Blade had turned about in his saddle and was firing back at Dena. She was standing in her stirrups with him in her rifle sights. She fired, and Sam Blade screeched and grabbed the side of his head. Hell, Fargo thought. She'd shot off his earlobe. She could kill him with one shot if she wanted. She fired again, and Blade grabbed his elbow as his rifle fell from his hand. In another second his horse passed under a tree. A low branch caught the back of Blade's head, and his body lifted out of the saddle. There was a hideous scream, and he hung for a second from the branch, then his body dropped heavily to the earth. Dena reined in, then heard Fargo approaching behind her. She whirled about with her rifle raised, then her face broke into wrinkled smiles as she recognized him.

"Fargo, you son-of-a-gun," she said. "I'm glad to see you in one piece." They sat on their horses for a moment, looking down at the corpse of Sam

Blade. There was a long silence between them, and then Fargo told her the answer to the question she wasn't asking him—about how Pete died. A tear ran down her leathery face. "I wish I really knew that man sooner," she said. She suddenly brought up her rifle and fired a shot into Sam Blade's head. The body jerked at the impact. "And I wish you'd died slower." Dena turned about and rode back toward the plain. Fargo followed.

They sat on the ridge, looking down at the battlefield. Corpses of horses and men lay scattered about. Sheriff Sikes himself was tending to Pauline's leg wound while the rest of the posse was rounding up the tattered remnants of Sam Blade's gang.

"You see, that ambush at the fork wasn't Blade at all," Dena explained. "It was Sikes. He'd got suspicious of that Indian scout. So he figured something was up. When he saw us coming down the road that morning, he thought it was Blade, until he saw the children. They were chasing us to help us. Hell, I got us all the way into Hell's Picket before they caught up.

They rode down toward where the sheriff stood beside Pauline. He looked up at Fargo and extended his hand.

"I owe you a big apology, Mr. Fargo," Sikes said. He took off his hat and raked his fingers through his hair. "Damned sorry I almost hanged you. Been chasing you and this Lady Shootist all week, trying to set things right again." He reached into his deep jacket pocket and pulled out a leather holster with a knife. "Here's your knife back."

Fargo swung down from the Ovaro and staggered when his wounded leg hit the ground. He offered his hand to the sheriff, and they shook.

"Looks like I got another leg to tend to," said Sikes, rolling up his sleeve. "Sit down here next to Miz MacKenzie."

Pauline smiled at him, the worry lines easing in her face. Fargo put his arm around her as the sheriff cut the denim away from his leg wound.

"Julie, Jimmy, and Hanna are safe in Hell's Picket," she murmured. Tears ran down her face. "And with the gold we can start over. Get our ranch back, build up the herd."

Sheriff Sikes grimaced when he saw the deep wound in Fargo's thigh.

"Hell, I've gotta dig that bullet out." Sikes grimaced. "And it's gone deep. This is going to hurt like hell."

Fargo lay back on the grass, his arm around Pauline. Sure, it hurt like hell having somebody dig a piece of lead out of your thigh. But through his mind, over and over, he saw the picture of Sam Blade's horse galloping under the tree. Of Sam Blade's head snapping as the branch caught him in the neck. And of Sam Blade lying dead on the grass.

"Have at it, Sheriff," Fargo said. "I'm not going to feel a thing."

LOOKING FORWARD!
The following is the opening
section from the next novel in the exciting
Trailsman series from Signet:

THE TRAILSMAN #173
WASHINGTON WARPATH

1860, the remote region around Mt. St. Helens—
where few white men had ever been
and lived to tell about it . . .

Skye Fargo liked San Francisco.

At night a man could go for a stroll through the Barbary Coast district and run into more lovely ladies of the night on each block than he would encounter in entire cities back East. Tall ones, short ones, skinny ones, plump ones, most dressed in skimpy outfits which would get them arrested if they dared show their cleavage in places like Omaha or Pittsburgh or Cincinnati. Redheads, blondes, brunettes, and raven-haired doves were there for the asking, and the right price.

It made Fargo's head swim to see so much natural beauty parading around like fillies at a stud farm.

The heady scent of mingled perfumes was downright intoxicating. All the big man with the lake blue eyes had to do was turn in a different direction and another wafting fragrance tingled his nostrils. It was like being in a flower shop, only better.

Skye Fargo was going to treat himself. He had spent the past week carrying a dispatch for the army from Carson City to the coast. Along the way he'd had to evade uppity Paiutes, convince a mountain lion that his horse would make a lousy meal, and blow the head off a rattler trying to turn his leg into a pincushion. He deserved a night of fun and frolic.

So far, though, Fargo had not set eyes on the right woman. Several had appealed to him in one way or another, but none had caused that telltale twitching in his loins which told him that they would do to spend the night with.

Fargo liked a certain carefree quality in his females. He wanted a beauty with a sparkle in her eyes and a genuine zest for life, one who would be all over him like a bear on honey and wear him out with her under-the-cover antics.

Then the Trailsman saw her.

A striking blonde stood on the corner of Kearny Street. Her dress, if you could call it that, was made from the sheerest fabric the big man had ever seen. It covered her from chin to ankles yet clearly revealed every square inch of her feminine charms underneath. The fact she was wearing no underclothes at all except for lacy panties helped.

But it was the woman's attitude and posture, more than her outrageous attire, which made

Fargo stop. Her smooth features were crinkled in a friendly smile, and she held herself tall and proud. Her back resting on the brick wall of an office building, she gazed on every man who went by, her frank invitation as plain as the cherry red lips on her face.

Fargo saw her glance at him, saw her blink and stiffen as if in surprise. Hooking his thumbs in his belt, he strolled over and remarked, "Never move to Denver. You'd freeze to death in two seconds wearing an outfit like that."

"Thanks for the advice, handsome," the blonde responded playfully in a sultry voice that brought a lump to Fargo's throat. She studied him from head to toe. "Buckskins and boots and spurs. Something tells me that you're not from around here."

"Only staying the night," Fargo said, "and I'm looking for some company. You interested?"

"The name is Greta." She straightened and stood so close to him that his chest nearly brushed her ample bosom. "Yes, I am. What did you have in mind?"

"A hot meal, a few drinks, and a room at the finest hotel in this part of town," Fargo detailed. "Since you must know San Francisco a lot better than I do, I'll let you be my guide."

Grinning, Greta went to take Fargo's arm, but she froze when her eyes drifted over his shoulder. Pivoting on a heel, Fargo discovered a lean, sallow man crossing the street toward them. Grungy clothes covered the newcomer's lanky frame, and his hair had been slicked back with grease. Fargo took an instant dislike to him.

"There you are, damn it!" the ratty man hailed the blonde. "Bruno had me lookin' all over for you, Greta. He wants to see you right this minute."

The woman's cheeks flushed with annoyance. "I'm not his dog, Wenckus. I don't come running every time he whistles. You go tell him that I'm busy, that I'll be there when I'm good and ready."

Wenckus made a clucking sound. "Tell him yourself, gorgeous. You know as well as I do that he's liable to pop a cork. And I'm not takin' the heat. So let's get going." Grasping her wrist, he started to walk off, but Greta wouldn't budge. "Didn't you hear me?" he growled. "Bruno wants you *now*."

Fargo had heard enough. It was plain the woman didn't care to oblige, and he was eager to go fill his belly with a heaping plate of lobster and shrimp. He liked seafood but rarely had an opportunity to indulge himself. Taking a step, he put his hand on the man's arm and said forcefully, "You heard the lady, mister. Let her be."

Wenckus jerked his arm loose and hissed like a riled sidewinder. "Who the hell are you? Didn't your pa ever tell you it's bad manners to stick your nose where it doesn't belong? Get lost, hick, before I decide to carve you up into little pieces."

Fargo hit him. He flicked a quick jab which staggered the ratty man backward. Wenckus dug in his feet, swayed, shook his head, and touched the trickle of blood seeping from the left corner of his mouth.

"Damn you, you bastard! I'll kill you for this!"

A knife blade flashed in the dim light. Fargo crouched as Wenckus came at him. He dodged a wild swing, ducked a low swipe. Enraged, Wenckus thrust, overextending himself, and Fargo seized the man's arm, slammed his knee into the elbow, and heard a gratifying snap. It provoked a screech of sheer agony. The knife clattered to the walk, and Wenckus pressed his clipped wing to his side.

"Son of a bitch!"

"Maybe now you'll take the hint," Fargo suggested. Gripping Greta's elbow, he turned to depart, keeping one eye on the shifty rodent. He was glad he did.

Uttering a high-pitched shriek, Wenckus launched himself at Fargo, kicking out with a heavy black boot. He aimed the blow at Fargo's spine, but the big man danced out of harm's way, shifted, and delivered an uppercut which lifted Wenckus off his feet and sent him crashing onto his back a few feet away. Groaning, the ratty man attempted to sit up. Fargo cocked his leg and planted his foot on the tip of Wenckus's jaw. That did the trick.

People had stopped whatever they were doing to stare. A few were hurrying over to see what the fuss was about. Since Fargo had no desire to tangle with the local law, he hastened off with the ravishing blonde at his side. She never said a word until several blocks were behind them.

"You shouldn't have done that, mister."

Fargo shrugged. "The name is Skye. And he was a pain in the ass. I bet people do it to him all the time."

"That's not what I meant. Wenckus works for Bruno Scaglia, and Bruno is not the sort of guy you want to have mad at you. He has his fingers in every racket on the Barbary Coast. If he wants someone dead, all he has to do is snap his fingers and they wind up on the bottom of San Francisco Bay."

"Why did you buck him, then?"

Her lovely face clouded. "Bruno thinks I'm his woman. He took a liking to me a while back and hasn't given me a moment's peace ever since, even though I've told him again and again that I don't want to see him. He just can't take no for an answer."

"Forget about him. You're with me tonight, and I'm not about to let anyone spoil our evening. Relax and enjoy yourself."

Greta pursed her lips, chuckled, and nodded. "All right. The least I can do to thank you for sparing me another night of hell with Bruno is treat you to a good time the likes of which you won't ever forget."

"Lead on."

The blonde steered Fargo down to the wharf at the north end of the waterfront. There, in a fancy restaurant decorated with anchors, boat wheels, and even large nets, they were treated to a feast fit for a king. Fargo relished every morsel of juicy lobster and the succulent shrimp meat. He dipped each piece in thick butter before rolling it on his tongue to savor the taste.

His escort watched him in amusement. About halfway through the meal she laughed and declared, "I don't think I've ever seen anyone take so much pleasure in eating before. Are you half starved?"

Fargo shook his head. "You're looking at a man who gets by on beef, venison, and jerky most of the time. This is a treat for me. And so is this." Picking up the tall glass of wine, he gulped and smacked his lips. "It's not coffin varnish, but I can't complain."

"Coffin varnish?"

"That's how some folks in Texas describe good sipping whiskey. If it can't put a shine on a casket or hair on a frog, it's not worth the bother."

Her gay mirth pealed through the room. "I take it you've seen a lot of the country, Skye?"

"More than most," Fargo admitted. At her prompting, he told about some of his far-flung travels, from the Everglades of Florida to the deep woods of remote Canada, from the arid deserts in Arizona to the pristine peaks of Montana. She listened intently, fascinated, and between the two of them they polished off two bottles of wine and began in on a third.

The meal made Fargo sluggish. It had been so long since he gorged himself that his body did not know how to handle it. The wine, which he regarded as little more than colored water, was more potent than he had counted on. By the third bottle he kept hearing an odd buzz in his ears, and he was pleasantly tipsy.

After the big man paid, they ambled out onto a pier and watched the lights of a ship in the distance. A brisk breeze from the northwest fanned Fargo's brow and cooled him down. The sight of Greta, her lush body outlined against the backdrop of tranquil ocean, had the opposite effect. Pulling her close, he touched his lips to hers. They were as soft as silk, as tasty as peaches smothered in sugar. Her smooth tongue glided into his mouth, entwining with his. For all of a minute they were locked in a tight embrace. When they parted, Fargo swore that his blood was pounding a drumbeat in his veins.

"Ummmm. That was nice," Greta said. "I can't wait to get to a hotel."

"Then what are we waiting for?" Fargo responded. He had money to spare which was burning a hole in his pocket. Looping an arm around her slender waist, he swiveled toward shore. And promptly froze.

A pair of brawny men stood at the other end of the pier as if waiting for them.

"Oh, no," Greta said softly. "I knew this would happen. Bruno has eyes and ears everywhere."

Fargo led her toward shore. Since it was against the law for a man to parade around with a pistol strapped to his hip in San Francisco, Fargo had tucked his up under his shirt and wedged it under his belt over his left hip, butt forward for a swift draw. He loosened his shirt now as he approached the burly longshoremen, who moved to bar his path.

"Bruno Scaglia wants to have a word with you, friend," stated the oldest of the duo. "You and the lady both. You're to come with us."

"No."

The men exchanged glances, and the older one said, "Maybe your ears don't work so good. What Mr. Scaglia wants, Mr. Scaglia gets. Make this easy on yourself." To accent his point, he bunched his ham-sized right fist and smacked it into his callused left palm with a sharp crack. "Hear that?"

Fargo produced the Colt with a flourish and twirled it front and back. Suddenly leveling it at the speaker, he cocked the hammer, retorting, "Hear this?"

At the metallic rasp both men tensed. The younger one took a step to the rear and raised both hands as if to ward off a slug.

"Go tell Mr. Scaglia that the lady and I have other plans," Fargo said coldly. "And let him know that I don't want to be bothered again. I have a short fuse, and he's mighty close to setting it off."

The talkative one scowled as he retreated into the night, saying, "This ain't over, mister. Not by a long shot. We'll pass on what you said, but Mr. Scaglia doesn't back down from anyone. You'll see."

Fargo hefted the pistol and smiled as the pair hustled into the darkness. Only when they had rounded a far corner and disappeared did he tuck the six-shooter back under his shirt and cover it. His companion stared at him in wide-eyed wonder.

"Aren't you just full of surprises!" Greta commented. "What are you? A desperado of some kind?"

Resuming their stroll, Fargo answered, "I don't make a habit of breaking the law unless it's a law so stupid it deserves to be broken." He patted his shirt, insuring the revolver was in place. "To make ends meet, at one time or another I've worked as a scout, a wagon train guide, a tracker, and more."

"And you never get an urge to set down roots?"

"Not yet," Fargo said. "I was bit by the wanderlust bug before I turned sixteen. I haven't looked back since."

Greta sighed wistfully. "How I envy you. I wish to high heaven I could do like you, go where I please when I please. It sounds like the kind of life most people would give their eye teeth to have."

Making small talk, the Trailsman and the dove hiked toward the center of the city. The streets were alive with foot and wagon traffic. San Francisco, he had been told, never slept; the people were on the go twenty-four hours a day. And he believed it. Every so often he checked behind them, but there was no evidence of anyone shadowing them.

"I know an excellent hotel called the Concord House," Greta revealed. "It's pricey, and it should be. They have thick red carpet in each room and big beds with mirrors on the wall. Room service will bring up a three-course meal. And they have the freshest-smelling soap in the world."

Fargo gave her bottom a lusty slap. It didn't matter to him where they spent the night. In his view one bed was as good as another. "If that's where you want to go, then the Concord House it is."

They turned into Portsmouth Square, the pulsing hub of San Francisco's gambling resorts, as casinos were commonly called. Although the city fathers were making a lot of noise in the local papers about clamping down on vice, the police seldom bothered to raid a casino, nor had they closed a single one down.

Portsmouth Square was lined with one den of iniquity after another. Prestigious places like the El Dorado and the Bella Donna were known as the cream of the crop. No expense had been spared to turn them into the most splendid establishments of their kind anywhere in the world.

The square was thronged with those who favored the city's night life. Men in expensive suits mingled with rough miners in dirty flannel shirts and shapeless hats. Mexicans wrapped in *serapes* leaned against walls, smoking their *cigaritas*. Women were fewer, but those present were dressed in exquisite dresses which showed off their bodies to perfection.

Skye Fargo found the swirl of activity intoxicating. He was strongly tempted to pay a visit to a poker table, but if he lost his poke he would be unable to afford the deluxe room Greta had her heart set on. As they wound through the stream of humanity, a female voice abruptly squealed Greta's name. From out of the doorway of a gambling hall shot a shapely brunette in a blue dress who threw her arms around the blonde and raved over and over again about how glad she was to see her.

"This is one of my best friends, Blanche Cunnings," Greta explained when the other woman calmed down.

"Pleased to meet you, big man," Blanche said, her warm hand lingering in Fargo's much longer than was necessary. "Where has she been hiding you?"

Before Fargo could respond, the two women took to chatting in hushed tones. He tolerated their giggling and their coy looks as long as he could, then snatched Greta's hand and said, "It was nice to meet you. We have to be going."

"Hold on, Skye," Greta said. "Blanche just invited us to join her party here in the Sacramento. She says the men with her won't mind, and we can have free drinks while we watch them play. What do you say?"

Spending time with a bunch of strangers was the last thing Fargo wanted to do, but he was reluctant to disappoint Greta. As if she could read his thoughts, she squeezed his hand and pecked him on the cheek.

"Please? For me. We won't be long. I promise. It's just that I haven't seen her in weeks, and we have catching up to do."

"Just so the free drinks are whiskey," Fargo grumbled, and nodded. The women pounced on him as if he were the prize at a raffle drawing and whisked him indoors. Right away a smoky haze enveloped them, and the strong scent of alcohol filled the air. So did the murmur of subdued talk which rose from the scores of players lining the tables along both walls and the hordes of onlookers packing the open spaces in between. There were so many people that it was a chore to elbow through to the faro table, where the brunette's three refined friends wanted to play. None of the trio gave Fargo more than a casual glance.

Fargo did not stay there long. The women were huddled to one side, ignoring him, so he shouldered his way to the bar and was waited on by a portly man in a white apron. His first sip of the whiskey sparked a contented sigh. It was the genuine article, not the watered down excuse for red-eye which many places sold.

Facing the room, Fargo leaned his elbows on

the edge of the counter and idly observed all that was going on. The most popular game was without a doubt faro, in which players bet on the values of cards as the dealers exposed them. At a table near him a man bet a stack of chips six inches high and never blinked an eye when he lost and the dealer raked them in.

A commotion broke out near the entrance. Half a dozen men had entered and were barreling their way through the crowd. In their lead was a mountain of a man as tall as he was wide, dressed in the very best suit money could by. Gold rings glittered on each finger, and he wore a gold watch chain as thick as a rope. Trailing him were two familiar faces: the longshoremen.

Instantly Fargo set down his whiskey and moved to intercept the hulking leader before the man reached Greta. He got there, but only a few steps ahead. The women were so busy gossiping that they hadn't noticed. Planting his feet wide, he declared, "You must be Scaglia."

The criminal kingpin regarded the Trailsman as if he were a bug fit to be squashed. "And you must be the son of a bitch who thinks he can get off with telling me what to do. Well, I'm here to show you the error of your ways, boy."

Fargo had his shirt tucked in. It would be impossible for him to unlimber the Colt before the roughnecks plowed into him. Trying to avoid trouble, he forced himself to stay calm and said, "I'm just looking to have a good time with the lady here. All we want is to be left in peace."

"Fat chance," Bruno Scaglia snapped, his fleshy cheeks and double chin quivering with fury. He swung the long, polished cane in his right hand. As he did, there was a click.

A blade four inches long popped out the tapered end, spearing at Fargo's throat. Only a desperate twist spared Fargo's life. He batted the cane aside, stepped in close, and delivered a solid punch to Scaglia's gut. It was like striking solid rock. His knuckles flared with pain.

Incredibly, the kingpin laughed, a low, rumbling sound like the snarling of a great bear. "Did you think that would hurt me, little man? Before I came to California and made my mark gambling, I used to work in a quarry in Ohio. From dawn to dusk six days a week I lifted boulders bigger than you. Ask anyone. You couldn't hurt me if you tried."

"Then you won't hold it against me if I make a liar out of you?" Fargo replied, even as he lifted his right boot and brought the heel down with all his might on the tip of Scaglia's left shoe.

The man's roar stopped every game in the gambling hall and drew all eyes to the towering figure who had lifted his hurt foot just as Fargo unleashed a roundhouse right which caught Bruno Scaglia on the right cheek and tottered him back into a table. The legs were unable to support his massive bulk. With a rending crash, kingpin and table smashed to the floor.

Scaglia floundered up and bellowed at his stunned men, "What the hell are you waiting for? *Nail the bastard!*"

The longshoremen were quick to obey. Lunging, they tackled Fargo as he tried to skip aside. Fargo winced as a fist caught him in the ribs. Another glanced off his chin. He was able to partly turn as he fell so that he wound up on his side with only one man on top of him. An elbow to the nose knocked the roughneck off. The second one drew back a fist, but Fargo slammed his forehead into the longshoreman's face, then rolled backward out of reach.

For a few moments Fargo was in the clear. Out of the corner of an eye he saw a gambler rise to protest the intrusion and be slammed flat by one of Scaglia's men. Another gambler leaped to the defense of the first, and another of Scaglia's cutthroats entered the fray. In a twinkling a dozen more men piled in, and the room erupted in savage violence.

Fargo lost sight of Greta and Blanche. The swirling melee also hid Bruno Scaglia. Thinking that he could get out of there without anyone being the wiser, he rose onto his hands and knees and started to crawl toward the bar. The next moment a shadow fell across him and he looked up to see a man in miner's clothes holding a chair overhead. "Now hold on," he said. "I'm not to blame—"

It was a waste of breath. The last sight Fargo saw was the chair sweeping down toward his head. Then a keg of black powder exploded in his skull, and a black cloud claimed his shattered senses.

FALCONER'S LAW
BY JASON MANNING

The year is 1837. The fur harvest that bred a generation of dauntless, daring mountain men is growing smaller. The only way for them to survive is the way westward, across the cruelest desert in the West, over the savage mountains, through hostile Indian territory, to a California of wealth, women, wine, and ruthless Mexican authorities.

Only one man can meet that brutal challenge—His name is Hugh Falconer—and his law is that of survival....

from **SIGNET**

WHISPERS OF THE RIVER
BY TOM HRON

They came from an Old West no longer wild and free—lured by tales of a fabulous gold strike in Alaska. They found a land of majestic beauty, but one more brutal than hell. Some found wealth beyond their wildest dreams, but most suffered death and despair. With this rush of brawling, lusting, striving humanity, walked Eli·Bonnet, a legendary lawman who dealt out justice with his gun ... and Hannah Twigg, a woman who dared death for love and everything for freedom. A magnificent saga filled with all the pain and glory of the Yukon's golden days....

from SIGNET